"With her graceful, captivating prose and exquisitely drawn characters, Annell López holds our hearts in her hand. *I'll Give You a Reason* is a self-assured, deeply compelling, absolutely stellar debut story collection."
—**JAMI ATTENBERG**, author of *The Middlesteins*

"*I'll Give You a Reason* captures the malaise of life when you can no longer predict what's ahead of you. But the stories in López's debut hum with something that might just be akin to hope."
—**IVELISSE RODRIGUEZ**, author of *Love War Stories*

"This collection is an instant classic. In stories both intimate and expansive, López dazzles with striking tales of desire thwarted or fulfilled. By turns darkly comic and achingly poetic, this is one of the finest collections of stories ever written."
—**MAURICE CARLOS RUFFIN**, author of *The Ones Who Don't Say They Love You*

"Full of spunk and insights that sneak up on you, and with prose as clear and sharp as laser surgery, López possesses an uncanny ability to get inside the heads and hearts of all the players—opponents and allies alike—in stories about immigration, sexuality, gentrification, and that ever-elusive American dream."
—**CASSANDRA LANE**, author of *We Are Bridges: A Memoir*

"Through these elegant, poetic, and often devastating short stories, López explores both the profoundly familiar and the strange in everyday immigrant and working-class American life. *I'll Give You a Reason* is a rare page-turner of a collection: startlingly sensitive, oozing with compassion, and full of both gentle and explosive revelations about human nature, forgiveness, and the grace we sometimes fail to offer ourselves. I couldn't put this extraordinary book down."
—**NANCY JOOYOUN KIM**, author of *The Last Story of Mina Lee: A Novel*

"There's a sharp and captivating voice throughout each story and character navigating identity, gentrification, colorism, and much more through the immigrant lens. This unique voice echoes the type of storytelling that captivated me in my youth and which made me long for more of its kind."
—**LUPITA AQUINO**, book influencer

I'll Give You a Reason

STORIES

Annell López

THE FEMINIST PRESS
AT THE CITY UNIVERSITY OF NEW YORK
NEW YORK CITY

Published in 2024 by the Feminist Press
at the City University of New York
The Graduate Center
365 Fifth Avenue, Suite 5406
New York, NY 10016

feministpress.org

First Feminist Press edition 2024

 This book is supported in part by an award from the
National Endowment for the Arts.

This book is made possible by the New York State Council
on the Arts with the support of the Office of the Governor and the New York State Legislature.

First printing April 2024

Cover illustration by Layqa Nuna Yawar LLC
Cover design by Brooke Houghton
Text design by Drew Stevens

Library of Congress Cataloging-in-Publication Data
Names: López, Annell, author.
Title: I'll give you a reason : stories / Annell López.
Other titles: I'll give you a reason (Compilation)
Description: First Feminist Press edition. | New York City : The Feminist
  Press at the City University of New York, 2024.
Identifiers: LCCN 2023051889 (print) | LCCN 2023051890 (ebook) | ISBN
  9781558613126 (paperback) | ISBN 9781558613133 (ebook)
Subjects: LCSH: Immigrants--Fiction. | Dominican Americans--Fiction. |
  Newark (N.J.)--Fiction. | LCGFT: Short stories.
Classification: LCC PS3612.O5825 I45 2024 (print) | LCC PS3612.O5825
  (ebook) | DDC 813/.6--dc23/eng/20231115
LC record available at https://lccn.loc.gov/2023051889
LC ebook record available at https://lccn.loc.gov/2023051890

PRINTED IN THE UNITED STATES OF AMERICA

For Gregory and my family

Contents

CONTENTS

Great American Scream Machine

EVA WATCHED AS JAY TUGGED ON THE CHAIN SECURING the gates of the park's baseball field. Over the past few months, the soft turf behind the bleachers had become their spot. It was dark and secluded, but not far from the Dunkin' Donuts and the pizzeria's joint parking lot where their classmates would sit on the hoods of their decked-out Hondas laughing and blasting music. Hanging out at that spot, doing nothing, is how Eva lived her life—always at the periphery. Today the gate was locked, so they sat against the tree and drank from a bottle of vodka-spiked Gatorade.

She took a deep breath and tried to hold it, hoping it would expand and fill the vast spaces inside. On the opposite side of the park, a construction crew had been working on a new boardwalk across the soccer stadium. For years, the banks of the Passaic River had been deserted wasteland. It was a place nobody wanted, until now.

"You all right, bro?" Jay finally asked. That's how he spoke to her, peppering his sentences with "bro" and "dude" as if those words could help dissipate any inkling of romance.

Eva took a second to think about the question. Moments ago, before Jay got there, she had felt her world was over. "I don't know." She tilted her head back and sipped from the Gatorade bottle. "Guess what?" she said.

"Needs more vodka?"

"Yes," she said. "But that's not it."

"What is it?"

"I'm an illegal," she said, before erupting into laughter.

He looked confused. "Illegal how?"

"Illegal as in no tengo papeles."

"Wait. You mean undocumented?"

Saying those words aloud made them feel even more real. She nodded, then covered her mouth with both hands. She didn't want to sob—not in front of Jay. He wouldn't console her. And he wouldn't understand; his family had been here for generations.

That morning she'd scavenged for her birth certificate after seeing a clip on the news about President Obama's. She heard about the citizenship conspiracy theory everywhere she went lately. At the coffee shop near her house, the women behind the counter argued about it. And she'd heard about it in the hallway across from the teachers' lounge: Mr. Jarrett and Mr. Zolinski, standing by the water cooler as usual, volleyed back and forth about the significance this piece of paper held over everyone's lives. Every now and then she'd recall their conversation, and that morning she couldn't shake the feeling that something was wrong. She'd paced around, thinking about how she had never seen her birth certificate—that little piece of paper that held so much power.

It was underneath her parents' bed in a lockbox, a charcoal rectangle purported to be indestructible. She'd sat on the edge of the bed, fiddling with the lock until she tried her birthday, the correct three-number combination. The twins' certificates were at the very top, still crisp. Hers was at the bottom, a yellowed and weathered piece of paper folded inside a Ziploc bag.

She'd held it closer to her face to make sure it wasn't a figment of her imagination. She'd run her fingers along the creases where it had been folded so many times. Everything was a lie: She hadn't been born at University Hospital on Market Street; she had been born in a clinic in Santo Domingo and was undocumented. Just like her parents. Just like the Ecuadorian lady who'd take bottles and cans from the recycling bins to trade them somewhere for five cents apiece.

Jay grabbed the bottle of Gatorade, poured more vodka into it, then shook it. "My dad is gay," he said, breaking the silence.

Eva thought it was a weird thing to say, and a weird time to say it—as if he needed to bring an offering to their misery junction. She thought of his parents, how uncomplicated they seemed. She had met them a few times. His mom was a bank teller at the Garden State Bank, and his dad owned a small plumbing business. They were nice, average people who did average things.

She cleared her throat. "Why do you think he's gay?"

"I'm sure of it," he said. "After school a couple of

days ago, I sat down at the computer to work on my research paper. Anyway, his email was open. He had just responded to an ad on Craigslist. Someone looking for dick." He paused and took a sip of Gatorade. "You know, I knew something was up. A while back he started going on these weekend-long fishing trips . . . and, like, I've never seen the man fish in his life. He doesn't even own fishing equipment. You don't just pick up fishing out of nowhere, you know?"

She didn't know whether people picked up fishing out of nowhere. Her parents didn't have any hobbies. They didn't go anywhere or do much of anything. They smelled like Bengay and cooking oil even on days when they weren't working. Her dad had a limp he nursed with ice every single night. Her mom's forehead had been burnt to a crisp by a bright overhead lamp at the factory where she used to sew dresses before she started cooking at the diner. Her parents worked and worked and worked.

"I'm sorry," she said to Jay.

"It's all good. I don't really care anyway. Everyone has their secrets, I guess."

She thought of the birth certificate. There was no way her parents could have managed to keep it a secret from her much longer. She would soon be eighteen, and even though she wasn't planning to go to college, she'd get a job at the mall or at the new hotel downtown one day and she would need documents to apply.

Jay grabbed her hands. "I'm sorry you're an illegal," he added. "I guess we shouldn't be here."

"Why not?" asked Eva.

"Don't you have to lay low or something?"

"I said I was undocumented. Not a fugitive."

But even though she said it, she didn't believe there was a difference. She'd seen how her parents lived. They owned very little. They couldn't travel anywhere. They couldn't even move to a better apartment. And even when they refused to speak about it, fear loomed over their lives. They lived in the shadows, peeking into the light only when it was safe.

Eva stared at the Honda Civics across the street and recognized the girls leaning on the cars. They had played tennis with her in Branch Brook Park for the two weeks she was a high school athlete, after her mom had nagged her about never joining anything. The girls had made her pick up all the tennis balls after practice. It hadn't felt like hazing, more like a rite of passage. But since her backhand sucked, she'd decided tennis wasn't for her. No after-school activity was. She had neither the interest nor the energy to do anything. If she could spend her days sleeping or watching Adult Swim, she would. But for some reason, hearing the girls' laughter rise above the passing traffic, she was hit with nostalgia. She felt homesick for all the missed opportunities to laugh with the same abandon. All that time wasted, she thought.

"What do you think they're laughing at?" she asked Jay.

"Some dumb shit, most likely."

"I could use some dumb shit right now."

"You want to go over there?" he asked.

Eva shrugged. "I don't know. I guess I'm curious."

"About what? They're doing the same shit we're doing."

"Drinking vodka mixed with Gatorade?"

"Maybe rum. But who cares?"

She'd never cared before. She lived her life like a dull knife, or like a muscle atrophied from never being used. Maybe that was the problem. If she'd cared enough to apply to colleges, or to a job other than her babysitting gig, maybe she would have found out about the birth certificate sooner. She would have confronted her parents, asked if they had a plan.

"Don't you want to know?" she asked, slurring. "Aren't you a little, itty-bitty bit curious?"

He grabbed her arm. "You want to know what's itty bitty?" He placed his other hand over her left breast, then giggled.

She shoved him off. "You know what? I don't think those guys across the street think I have itty-bitty titties, Jay." She used his knee to push herself up. She walked over to the sidewalk and lifted up her shirt and bra in one fell swoop. The cold breeze brushed against her brown nipples. She jumped up and down and laughed, and for a moment she felt excitement coursing through her.

Jay walked over to her, shaking his head. "Are you okay?" he asked, putting a hand on her shoulder.

She wasn't. Everything her parents had feared now seemed so real. Raids and deportation were not mere phobias anymore. She wanted to stop thinking about it. "I'm great." She looked at the crossing sign. Fifteen seconds left. "Let's go," she said. Though the kids across the street were not her friends, they greeted her with effusive side hugs, as if they had known her forever. "Damn, girl. You're crazy," a girl shouted from the front seat of one of their cars. Eva smiled and nodded, then swiveled to take in the scene. Pizza boxes were strewn across the hoods of two Honda Civics, and smoke from Black & Milds and vapes billowed in the air. Standing on this side of the street was more exciting than anything she'd done in months.

"I'm Eva," she said to a few of the faces surrounding her.

"Eva!" one of her classmates called out. "Paco and Isaac took out their cell phones to record you, but then you put your shirt down, so they didn't get anything," she added.

The girl didn't introduce herself and Eva couldn't remember her name. Eva observed the girl's denim jacket; pink wool lined the collar and edges of the pockets. It looked like a jacket she'd once wanted but her parents couldn't afford. Both Paco and Isaac were in her music class. The two of them sat together in the back and texted during most of class. She had noticed Paco the way you notice something pretty in passing.

Paco shook his head. "No, I wasn't trying to do that." He took a drag from his vape, then exhaled. Bubble gum–scented vapor filled the air between them.

"I don't care," said Eva.

Paco's eyes widened.

"What I meant was—"

"I know what you meant," he said. He took another drag before passing the vape to her. She parted her lips and inhaled. From the corner of her eye, she noticed Jay watching her.

"Is that your boyfriend?" Paco asked.

"Who?" she said. "Jay? Not really."

She and Jay were friends who shared each other's apathy. Friends who occasionally had sex. The first time they slept together, they had been watching *Jeopardy* in his room. He pushed against her slowly, frequently checking in to make sure she was okay. In her head, she was answering *Jeopardy* questions. She hadn't planned to have sex with Jay that day. Neither of them was the kind of person who planned anything. It lasted a few minutes and she didn't think anything of it. She was as unmoved by sex as she was by everything else.

"You hungry?" Paco asked, pointing at the droopy slices of pizza.

If she were to be deported, she thought, she would miss the pizza most. She hadn't been much of anywhere, so she wondered where else in the world you could eat pizza like this. She grabbed a slice and took a bite.

She stared at Paco's face. All of his features were proportionate to one another. A sketch of symmetry. "So what's the plan for tonight?" she asked.

He opened the door to his car. "We were just going to smoke and chill. It's Mischief Night. Not tryna be out here too long."

"Nothing ever happens on Mischief Night," she said. "But then again I'm always home, so I don't really know."

"Yeah, not much," he said. "Just eggs, toilet paper, gang initiation, gunshots."

She laughed. "That shit doesn't happen here anymore. Not since all the white people came."

"Excuse me, miss. It's called gentrification." He grabbed her empty plate and her napkin, then winked at her.

She turned around and found Jay standing near her, orbiting like a satellite. Looking at Jay made her think of all the time they'd spent across the street doing nothing, talking about nothing. And then sometimes he'd wear khaki pants and a buttoned-up white shirt that made him look like he was ready to introduce you to his lord and savior Jesus Christ. She began to resent him, to wish she hadn't spent so much time with him. She wanted to cut whatever tethered him to her hip. She wanted to shake him off.

Different songs were blaring from a couple cars in the lot. The thundering bass made her feel disoriented. She tied her hair into a ponytail only to untie it seconds later. Her head was pounding.

She pulled her phone out of her pocket and saw that her parents had been calling her. She had been so devastated by the realization about her birth certificate that she hadn't let them know she wouldn't be home. She hadn't checked in with them in hours. She walked away from the crowd to listen to a voicemail. Though she was still angry, the sound of her mother's voice, splintering from agony, made her sad. She knew her parents would be worried sick about her; she wasn't normally the kind of kid who'd stay out late. And she knew there wasn't much they could do but wait for her—it's not like they could call the police to report their teenage daughter missing. And yet she still didn't call them back. She put the phone back in her pocket, not ready to face their anger. Not when she was still dealing with her own.

Eva stared at her reflection in a small puddle of fluid that had leaked from one of the parked cars. With the heel of her boot, she stomped on the silhouette of her hair. Tiny iridescent droplets splashed all over.

From the distance, her new friends called her over. Why had it taken her so long to want to be a part of something, albeit small—something as harmless as a group of friends hanging out on a Sunday night? She had been so aloof for so long, deliberately monochrome in a whirlwind of colors. She smiled at the group, wishing her worries would drift off elsewhere.

She walked over to Paco's car and sat inside. His car was mostly clean, except for a basketball and some sneakers on the back seat. She stretched her legs and reclined, gazing at the Little Tree air freshener dangling from the rearview mirror and its intense artificial vanilla scent. Outside, Paco and Jay gathered napkins and leftover pizza to throw in the trash. The girl who'd greeted her now sat with her friends in the back of a car parked next to Paco's. They were headbanging to Rihanna's "We Found Love." Underneath the noise, she felt fear thumping in her chest. Her phone kept vibrating. The more she thought about her parents, the more she dreaded answering their calls. What was she supposed to say?

What do you do when the bad things that happen to other people happen to you?

Paco approached the car. "Your boyfriend left," he said. She didn't respond; she just didn't care if Jay was there or not. He opened the door and sat on the driver's side. The rest of her classmates began pulling out of the parking lot.

Isaac yelled, "Yo, Paco! Text me," before rolling up his window.

Paco put his arm around the back of the passenger seat and moved closer. "So what do you want to do?"

"What's there to do?" she asked. "Don't you guys race cars or something?"

"Do you even live here? We don't race anymore," he said. "Not since they built those speed bumps all over the neighborhood."

"You mean gentrification," she teased.

He laughed. "We can go to Erika's." Erika's house was a good place to chill, he explained. Her dad had just sold his car, so their garage was empty save for some boxes of food and clothing meant to be shipped to relatives in Brazil. The only caveats were that people had to park blocks away on some other street so as not to raise her parents' suspicion, and that Talia, the other Brazilian of the bunch, had to follow Erika upstairs to greet her mom so the rest of them could sneak into the garage.

THEY SAT IN a circle on the ground in Erika's garage— thigh to thigh, elbow to elbow. The girls complained that it was cold. The boys asked, almost collectively, if their nipples were hard, claiming it was the only way to tell.

The girl with the denim jacket, all chirpy and breathless, said they should all play Never Have I Ever.

"I'm sure we could play something better," said Isaac. "Like Truth or Dare."

Paco chimed in, "Or Never-Have-I-Ever-Truth-or-Dare."

"Is that even a real game?" Eva asked.

He put his hand on her knee. It was large enough to palm a basketball. The warmth radiating from his touch was comforting and exciting. She inched closer to his body, seeking that warmth. She smiled at him and he smiled at her, his hand still lingering.

"Anything in this world is possible," he said. He'd obviously meant it sarcastically, but in the darkness of a stranger's garage, with despair churning inside her, Eva wanted those words to be prophetic, for Paco to be a harbinger of hope.

Across from Eva, the girl with the denim jacket tapped her foot against the ground repeatedly. "What's taking them so long?" she asked.

"Who?" asked Eva. "Oh, you mean Erika and Talia?" She had forgotten that the girls were still upstairs. "Did we get them in trouble?" She turned to Paco once again, like he was her personal excursion guide.

"No," he said. "They're just being polite. Erika's mom is chill, but every now and then she just wants to know who Erika hangs with, you know."

"Makes sense," Eva said, though she couldn't relate.

Her parents didn't know her friends. For one, she didn't have many.

"We should play something while we wait," said the girl with the denim jacket. She inched forward, then called out to Paco: "Fuck, Marry, Kill. Your choices are Eva, Isaac, and me."

Isaac, who had been on his phone, looked up at Paco. "You better not let me down, son."

They all laughed, and Paco blushed. "Damn, Mia. Why you putting me on the spot like that?"

Eva stared at the dimple on his left cheek. It was deep, like the divot of a thumbprint cookie. She wanted to trace it with her fingers.

"Fine," he continued. "I'd marry Isaac, kill Mia, and fuck Eva."

The thought sent a rush to the pit of Eva's stomach, but it quickly disappeared. She considered that she might not be around long enough for that to happen. At any point there could be a raid. Though she hadn't seen one in real life, her parents talked about them in whispers, crossing themselves, repelling those thoughts with a "God forbid" and a prayer.

Eva cleared her throat and interrupted everyone's laughter. "Let's play Never Have I Ever."

She heard footsteps behind her. Erika returned, balancing a stack of plastic cups. Talia followed, cradling a space heater and snacks. They set everything on the floor. Eva grabbed a cup and poured herself some vodka from the plastic bottle going around.

"Never Have I Ever," she started, "left the country."

Almost in unison, everyone around her sipped from their cups. She stared at everyone, registering how they all stared at her. "Really?" asked Isaac. "Not even to visit your family?"

"Nope." She knew her parents couldn't go back, even if they wanted to. They rarely ventured outside city limits. Leaving the country was out of the question. The DR mystified her. She only knew what she had seen in photographs and travel ads, and the version from her parents' stories, filtered through their experiences. They had grown up poor. They had struggled. The thought of getting deported there scared her.

Trying to keep it together, she tilted her head and gulped from her cup. Paco grabbed the cup out of her hand, then leaned in closer.

"Save some for the rest of the game, lady," Paco whispered in her ear.

Eva felt Mia's gaze from across the circle. She wondered if Mia had noticed her looking at her denim jacket. When Eva caught Mia staring again, she smiled but Mia didn't smile back. Before today they hadn't interacted much. "Never Have I Ever flashed my tits in public," Mia said, looking at Eva.

"They're just tits," Eva shrugged. "We've all seen tits before."

"So you've never sent nudes before?" asked Isaac.

"Nope," Mia said. "What can I say? I'm not a thot."

Eva laughed. Never had she ever been in a squabble. But tonight was a night of firsts. She imagined crawling over to Mia and slapping her, leaving a red handprint on her pale face and taking her damn jacket. That would only bring some temporary relief, however, before snowballing into a major situation, the avalanche of consequences crushing her. That'd definitely get her deported.

"Don't do that, Mia," Paco said.

Mia rolled her eyes. "Why is she even here?"

Eva had asked herself the same question and kept arriving at the same answer: Why not? Why not be there? Why not be in all the places doing all the things for as long as she could before being shipped back like damaged goods?

When the game ran its course, her classmates talked about what they would do after high school. Eva thought she could clean houses in Manhattan or Hoboken, if she could find the right people willing to pay her under the table. Maybe she would teach herself how to cook. She could continue to babysit, maybe venture out to other cities. People in Montclair had money and jobs and lofty goals that often required others to care for their children. Or maybe she could marry somebody. One of those older Portuguese men. One with American citizenship. But there were thousands of girls just like her in the four square miles of the Ironbound. Many of them were prettier, she thought. There was also the church; maybe she would become a nun. But then what if . . . what if she did something so grand, so magnificent, that nobody cared about her papers? Or what if the world changed? What if in a few years, none of this mattered?

She whispered in Paco's ear, asking him if they could leave. She'd had enough of the party.

"Do you want me to take you home?" he asked.

"Not ready to go home yet," she said, though her parents were still texting her.

THEY PARKED IN one of the industrial backstreets of the Ironbound near an abandoned warehouse. It was 9 p.m. and both her mother and father would be home after their long shifts. She pictured them sitting on the living room couch, its collapsed vertebrae hidden under sagging fabric, an eyesore that swallowed anyone who sat on it.

She unbuckled her seatbelt and stretched until she heard the bones in her chest pop. She cracked open the window. It was chilly outside, but she needed some fresh air. The air freshener was suffocating her. At her insistence, they got out of the car and began walking in the street, alongside the curb.

"This is so different at night," she said.

"Yeah," Paco said. "No illegals looking for construction work this late."

The word made her flinch, the sound of it sharp and piercing like the whistle of a kettle. She wrinkled her mouth.

"What?" he said. "My dad used to come here for work when I was little. Now he owns his own roofing company. It all worked out." He turned to face her, then took a step back. If he had tried to lean in for a kiss, she would have dodged it. The word had unsettled her that much.

"It's Mischief Night," he said, picking up a rock from the ground and throwing it at the warehouse. He aimed for the glass window but missed by a few inches.

"Let me try," Eva said. She picked up a rock and flung it as hard as she could. It pierced a hole right through the window. The sound of glass shattering brought her a sense of release she hadn't expected. She bent over to gather more rocks.

He shook his head. "You're crazy."

"I'm all right," she said, squaring up and drawing her arm back. She threw the rock and then another, shattering each glass pane. She picked up more rocks and threw them at the building, a trash can, the barbed-wire fence, a parked car, and at the ground till she was out of breath.

"Are you okay?" he asked. She paused but didn't respond.

She screamed: a full-throated shriek that echoed and made her feel something other than grief, that reminded her of how, years ago at Six Flags, she'd sat in the front row gripping the metal bar of the Great American Scream Machine. For just a moment, it felt like she had been suspended in the air, squeezing the metal rail. She could only hear the slow, steady creaking of the roller coaster as it reached its peak, and then a visceral shrill erupting from inside her, loud and sharp, above everyone else's screams.

Nearby an alarm blared. "Fuck. We gotta go," Paco said.

They bolted, kicking up gravel as they ran past the corner until they made it to his car. Paco unlocked the door and plopped into the driver's seat, breathless. Eva didn't get inside. She stood next to the car and stared at the warehouse, with its red brick walls and braids of ivy. It looked captivating, as if its state of disarray was by design. In the right light, Eva thought, everything changes: the rat-infested banks of the Passaic River would soon become a boardwalk, and this blighted, abandoned warehouse, as ethereal as a portal to a different dimension, could, too, become something else. What if she didn't have to live a life on the margins, like scribbles on the side of a page? What if this wasn't the end of the world? What if life was as ugly as it was beautiful, as bleak as it was hopeful?

Dark Vader

I WAS REGISTERING FOR THE GED WHEN JUNIE STORMED into the house, slamming the door behind her. Her heavy *Princess and the Frog* backpack fell off her shoulder; the drop made the hardwood floors of our walk-up tremble.

"That was a bit dramatic," I said. But she didn't laugh. I closed my computer even though I wanted to finish registering for the test. The way Junie came in made me feel like I needed to give her my attention.

She threw her bubble coat onto the couch, then removed her snow boots, socks and all.

"They keep calling me Dark Vader," she said.

"What?"

"Dark Vader! Every time they see me, they giggle and say Dark Vader."

She took a deep breath, then slowly released a lungful of air, the way our mother taught her. The way I couldn't figure out how to when I was her age. She looked at me. "Who is Dark Vader?"

"You mean Darth Vader?"

"No. Dark with a *k*."

I pinched my nose like I was trying to stifle a sneeze. But truthfully I was trying to stop myself from laughing at the fucked-up ways kids were inventive. Junie was eight, too young to know who Darth Vader was, or to own a smartphone to look him up on—not that it stopped her from begging for one. I opened a browser on the laptop. Junie stood behind me, puffs of her banana Laffy Taffy breath brushing my cheek.

"That's Darth Vader," I said.

I turned and watched her eyes shift from side to side. She was the spitting image of our mother, only much darker. I readied myself to hold her on my lap and explain the whole Darth Vader bullshit with as much empathy as possible. It wasn't the first time kids had baptized her with some catchy nickname. Last year, when she joined the dojo on Niagara Street, an older kid referred to her as Blackie Chan. Our mother refused to explain to her what it meant and instead allowed Junie to believe Blackie Chan was not only real, but so strong he could karate-chop cinder blocks in half. Our mother embellished the idea of this fictional Blackie Chan so much that Junie thought his strength came from his Blackness. She assumed, naturally, that the color of his skin needed to resemble that of his karate belt.

On the computer screen Darth Vader stood defiantly, holding a lightsaber in front of a crew of stormtroopers. Junie folded her arms at the indignity of it all. "I get it," she said. She shifted her gaze to the coffee table where my phone had started buzzing. "Your phone, Vanessa."

"I hear it."

"Who is 'M'?" she asked. "Is that Mami?"

"No."

It was Mateo. But he was my boss, fifteen years older, and still married. I couldn't bring myself to save his number under his actual name. I flipped the phone over. Junie looked at me.

"I'm sorry they're calling you names," I said. "Kids are stupid."

She shook her head. "Whatever. I don't care."

It was as if saying those words out loud made them true. Within seconds her expression softened. Then she smiled and lunged her arms at me. I embraced her. I was twenty-four and Junie was eight. Our sixteen-year age difference had warped our reality; I always felt like she was my daughter and not my little sister. It's what everyone thought, anyway. I had dropped out of high school one winter, and Junie was born the following spring. I hadn't even had a boyfriend at the time, but the variables were there, asking to be shaped into a narrative that made sense: Baby equals dropout. Dropout equals baby. If it walks like a duck, then it must be.

I've woken up from dreams where she is mine: dreams where I come out as a mother and all of a sudden I have an external reason for bettering myself—a human being whose needs wipe away my feelings of inadequacy, and the crippling anxiety that keeps me from passing the fucking GED.

She squeezed me tighter. "I love you," she said.

Our mother had named her after the month of June, which wasn't the month when Junie was born but the month our mother had trekked the Mona Passage from Santo Domingo to Puerto Rico by boat, eventually making her way to New Jersey. It took her the entire month of June to make it to Newark. So she named her second daughter Junie, to remind herself that America was for second chances.

"Junie," I whispered. "Want me to fuck somebody up?"

She giggled, then shushed me. "You're gonna get in trouble with Mami," she said.

Our mother hated my cursing, especially in front of Junie. But whether I cursed or not, my mother was usually angry at me. She had her reasons. Her anger, her disappointment, they went far beyond my lack of a high school diploma. I had betrayed her. I had spat on her American dream.

"Violence is never the answer," Junie added.

The same message had been relayed to me all throughout middle school. Not that it registered at the time. For as long as I could remember, everything would spark a flame in me, and I'd fan those flames until they engulfed me. By eighth grade I'd been in over a dozen fights, two of which landed me in long-term suspensions. I had a few souvenirs: a small scar at the corner of my right eye (from hitting the edge of the curb), a crooked ring finger (from punching a wall), and a shitty relationship with my mother (from all of the above).

Shortly before Junie was born, things got worse for me at school. In the winter of my junior year, I'd been sitting quietly in Ms. Gomez's biology lab when a beaker fell. I hadn't dropped it—at least I don't remember doing it. Not that it mattered then, because Ms. Gomez had stiffened up like one of her taxidermied birds and headed toward me, ready to humiliate me for something I hadn't done. Before I knew it, I'd struck her in the nose. Mami was too humiliated to attend any of the meetings that followed, so I never went back to school.

Junie wasn't like me. Junie didn't hold on to anger. Insults would slide off her like water down a glass window.

"When is Mami coming home?" she asked.

"I'm not sure."

Mami had picked up extra shifts. After our last fight—when she said my bartending job was ungodly—she refused to let me help out with bills. I had told her I'd gotten a new job at a law office above Penn Station; I no longer worked at that seedy tavern she hated so much. She'd said, "Doing what? You don't even have a high school diploma." No matter how hard I tried to talk to her about my new job, she wouldn't hear it.

We hadn't had a real conversation in weeks. We lived like roommates who could not stand each other and only spoke when it was absolutely necessary. Despite how much I had disappointed her, I made her life easier. Why couldn't she see that?

I wasn't lying to her. Mateo had gotten me a job as an office clerk after a speech about how he, too, was once poor, how his parents had come to the United States from Portugal with nothing but fifty-six dollars in their pockets. I'd asked him to calculate inflation and give me the real sum. He'd kissed my stomach and said that didn't fit the narrative.

At twenty dollars an hour, the job was the best thing someone like me could find. It was better than wearing an Elmo costume to pose with tourists in the middle of Times Square or, most recently, wearing a plunging neckline to pour Yuengling at the tavern where I'd met Mateo.

Behind us in our kitchen, the old furnace clanged and banged, warming the air. Junie picked up her coat and hat off the couch without my prompting. She took a stack of books from her backpack and set them on the table, then began to do her homework.

Though it was only five o'clock, the sun had already gone down. I resisted the urge to text Mami because if it wasn't about Junie, more often than not she would ignore me. There were leftovers in the fridge from a few days ago, a tray of Portuguese barbecue: some pieces of rotisserie chicken, yellow rice, and an overdressed salad of wilted iceberg lettuce and tomatoes.

Junie looked at me. "Mac and cheese?" she said. She was perfectly content eating the same lousy dish several days in a row. But I was taking holiday photos at my new job in two short days, so I refused to eat anything that would make my cheeks look puffier than they already were. "We need to expand your horizons, young lady."

"So pizza?"

I shook my head, but she insisted.

"Fine. I'll grab a smoothie for me and a slice for you."

She nodded in agreement, then went back to her homework.

"I'll be back in fifteen minutes. Don't move from that table."

I stopped at the foot of the stairs to check my phone, which kept vibrating in my pocket. One missed call, one voicemail, and a text message. All from Mateo. I opened his message: a picture of a bulge poking through the open zipper of his navy slacks.

Is that yours? I replied. I waited for him to respond. Forty wasn't that old, but for some reason it always took him forever to text back.

Your turn. Spread them for me, he texted.

I can't. I'm with Junie.

Can I see you tonight?

I don't know, I wrote. *It's not Thursday yet.*

It was his rule. A way, he'd told me, to exercise control at a time in his life when everything existed outside the lines. I wanted to believe he was telling the truth, that he was not still with his wife. Either way I thought it was endearing, the idea that we could control anything.

Downstairs, Ms. Maxwell, our neighbor from across the street, shoveled snow onto the parking spot in front of our apartment. I stopped next to it, keys in hand, and looked at her.

"I just need to move my car for a moment," she yelled. Her old Buick had been left in the same spot for weeks, but because she was a crossing guard and a friend of folks in high places in the city, her car had been left unbothered, even on street-cleaning days where cars left on the wrong side of the street were quickly towed away. I crossed the street. Wind whistled around me. Flurries of snow and bits of ice struck my cheeks like tiny daggers.

"I shoveled that spot for my mom," I said. She looked at me and nodded the way people do when they don't understand what's going on. She didn't hear a word I said.

"Excuse me, Ms. Maxwell, I shoveled that spot for my mom."

"Yeah, but you guys don't own that spot," she said. "You guys are renters, not homeowners, dear." She said it with a smile. In fact, she always spoke with a smile regardless of what came out of her mouth. Her dog ran out from inside the shed and stood at the gate, barking.

We were indeed just renting this apartment. People up and down this street had a way of making distinctions between who owned and who rented. She was right that the spot didn't belong to us, but it also belonged to no one. Besides, I had gone to the trouble of shoveling it.

"Can't you just pile the snow somewhere else?" I asked. Her dog was still barking, but she didn't even look his way.

"Where am I supposed to put it, sweetheart?" She smiled bigger this time, baring her optic-white dentures. All around us, piles of rock-hard snow stood tall, waist high. It had snowed weeks ago, and the sun hadn't shined hot enough to melt it since then. Ms. Maxwell was right that there wasn't anywhere else to put the new snow. Years ago I would have told her to shove it. But I wasn't that girl anymore.

"Do you really need to move your car? It's so dark and slippery," I said, smiling.

"All right, all right." She grabbed her shovel and headed back inside. Her dog followed.

I looked to the end of the street. People were returning home from work. They were salting and scraping and shoveling away, trying to make room for their cars. Suddenly the walk to the pizzeria and the café no longer felt like a good idea. I turned back to our place, then ran up the stairs.

Junie waited for me at the door. "I saw you talking to Ms. Maxwell. I watched you from the window."

"She was dumping snow on Mami's spot," I said.

"I don't like Ms. Maxwell," she said, and I couldn't help but think how much I didn't like Ms. Maxwell, either. The lady had been a crossing guard since the first coming of Jesus. She was a permanent fixture in the neighborhood. People came and went, things changed, but Ms. Maxwell was always there, reporting to the school the events she'd witnessed around the neighborhood: who had fought, who had stolen candy from the convenience store. She even knew who'd tried to sneak into the go-go bar blocks away from the school.

I took a deep breath. "Why don't you like her?"

Junie waited for a moment. It seemed as if she was trying to decide whether telling me was a good idea.

"I'm not gonna do anything to her," I said. "Trust me. If I really wanted to, I would have done so years ago."

"Okay," she started slowly. "I think she laughed when they called me Dark Vader."

"You think or you know?" I asked.

"Yeah, she laughed."

"Who's calling you Dark Vader, anyway? You haven't told me."

She paused and wrinkled her mouth, considering the question. "Dylan and Joseph."

"Ms. Maxwell's kids?"

"Grandkids," she corrected.

"Color me shocked."

"What?" she said.

"I'm not surprised."

She looked at me. Her eyes glistened and for a moment I wondered if there were tears waiting for permission to be released. She was, after all, just a baby; even if she was strong, even if she'd learn to cope with mean words, they had to be stored somewhere.

I looked at the clock. It was 6 p.m. Mami would be home soon, tired from twelve hours of smiling and standing in the cold outside the high-rise, opening doors for rich people in Jersey City.

I walked over to the pantry and grabbed a single-serving cup of mac and cheese and a handful of broccoli florets from the fridge and nuked both in the microwave.

"Eat all of it," I said to Junie.

I grabbed a hat and a pair of gloves, resolved to camp out in the cold to keep that parking spot open, however long it took. I laid a towel down on the stoop and felt the cold travel from the concrete through the fabric of my clothes to my skin.

I turned and saw my mother down the street, walking toward the apartment, holding her ridiculous bell cap with one hand. She looked silly, but she liked the job most days. The tips and Christmas bonuses made it worth her while.

"Why are you out here?" she said.

"I was saving the parking spot for you. Where's your car?"

She pushed the door open with her shoulder. "I took the train home."

"Well, yeah, obviously. But where's the car?"

She shook her head, then started up the stairs. It'd been a while since she could climb all three floors without stopping to catch her breath. Today she seemed hell-bent on making sure I saw how she could swiftly walk up without so much as a pause between floors.

"I left the car at the parking garage at work," she said. "It's too hard to find parking here."

"There was no need for that."

"How would I know that you were saving the spot for me?"

"Because you should know better. And also, you could just text me and ask."

"No, gracias."

I walked past her and straight into my room. There was so much I wanted to say to her, about Junie, about Mateo, about me. Instead I sat on the bed. I couldn't force her to speak to me regardless of how much I wanted her to know that, sure, my relationship with Mateo was problematic, but I was trying my best to get somewhere, to be something that'd make her journey to this country worth a damn.

I should have insisted that we talk, but it was easier

to move on. So I responded to Mateo's text instead. *What do you have in mind?* I wrote, though I already knew the answer.

THE HOTEL ROOM smelled like citrus and lavender. It wasn't pungent, but it was a bit much, and it made me wonder if the scent was meant to mask something else. Nondescript landscapes adorned the peach stucco walls: generic images printed on cheap canvas. The place was clean, but it wasn't necessarily nice.

Mateo kissed the back of my ear and traced his fingers along the nape of my neck, down to the small of my back. In a whisper, he asked if I was hungry and offered to order in. I told him I wasn't hungry. I didn't want food. Not when so much else was taking up space. What I wanted was to talk, but his zeal, his desperation, fizzed over like Coke spilling from a bottle that'd been shaken and shaken.

He kissed me again, then pulled me closer, his arms wrapping around me. I felt his penis harden against my lower back. He grabbed my hip firmly and flipped me over. Sliding his hand down my thigh, he grabbed me by the knee and pried my legs open. "Maybe you'll be hungry after this," he said.

He pushed his face between my thighs, drawing circles with his tongue. For a second, the world paused: the impending deadline for the GED, the holiday photos, my mother, Junie, Dark Vader; it all began to disappear. I felt myself dissolving like a sugar cube.

But then he stopped.

"What's wrong?" I asked.

"You're not making any noise." He wiped his mouth and nose on the sheets, then sat up at the foot of the bed.

"Why did you stop?" I asked.

"Because you didn't seem to be enjoying it."

"I was enjoying it. I just have a lot on my mind."

He took a deep breath. "Do you want to talk about it?" he asked, sounding deflated.

I didn't think I could. I didn't have the courage to tell him I no longer wanted to live in this nebulous space. I wasn't naive enough to delude myself into thinking I would ever be a wife or a girlfriend. Girls like me don't build castles out of sand. Regardless, I was getting tired of being the girl he'd drive to a hotel off the turnpike once a week.

"I'm okay," I said.

He began to kiss my calves. "Where were we?" he said, holding on to my ankles.

I stared at the one painting in the room that wasn't a landscape: a painting of the ocean, foamy waves crashing on the shore. It reminded me of my mother. To have crossed the Caribbean Sea on a boat, the sun, sea, and salt scorching her skin, only to get to the US and have a twenty-four-year-old directionless dropout for a daughter. What the fuck was I doing?

I grabbed a handful of Mateo's black hair and yanked it toward me. I moaned, even though I felt nothing.

MATEO LEFT THE room at the crack of dawn and didn't return. I woke up to several messages on my phone. He'd texted me heart emojis, along with an apology for disappearing. In a separate message he urged me to take the day off, to "get some much-needed rest." The room was already paid for and checkout was at eleven. But even if I'd tried, I couldn't have spent any more time in that room. The more I breathed the artificially scented air, the more I felt cheap, like the ceramic lamp resting on the plywood night table or the patterned rug or the artwork hanging on the walls. It all made me want to shed my skin.

The other messages were from my mom, reprimanding me for not texting her to let her know I'd be spending the night elsewhere. It surprised me. I'd been spending nights with Mateo for a while, and she had never seemed to care. She hadn't texted to check on me in months. For a long time it'd felt as if her only daughter was Junie, and I was just an appendage she was forced to carry. Her second message was a reminder that there was a GED bootcamp at the library. *I'll look into it*, I wrote.

I had failed the GED numerous times, but it was never because of the material. I could read a passage, then answer comprehension questions using supporting evidence. I could calculate how much a hypothetical housewife would have to pay for six hours of a carpet steamer that rents for $12.85 per hour. I could read and interpret a graph and a pie chart. What I couldn't do was stop the sweat from pooling in my palms. Or the stomach pains. Or the nausea. Or the panic attacks. I couldn't stop picturing my former high school classmates flipping their tassels from left to right and tossing their graduation caps in the air.

I checked out of the hotel, then went to the library like I'd told my mom I would. I sat in the front of the room. It wasn't my first time attending some remedial course to help me prepare for the test, but it was the first time in a long while that I felt a surge of hope. Just being there meant something. At the very least I could go back home and tell my mother I had gone, even if nothing came of it. Even if, in the end, I'd end up failing once more. At the very least I could tell her I tried.

The instructor, a young woman with at least a dozen beaded bracelets dangling from her wrist, began the class with a meditation exercise. She told us to close our eyes and imagine ourselves in the future. I looked around, perhaps expecting some defiance, but everyone kept their eyes closed, surrendering to the exercise. If it was good enough for them, it was good enough for me, so I closed my eyes even if I couldn't picture the future. After a minute or so, she suggested we introduce ourselves. She said if we knew more about one another, the reasons why we were there, we might be more likely to hold each other accountable. Though I wasn't looking forward to sharing anything about myself, I knew she was right.

At her urging, a couple folks stood up one after the other. A woman, probably in her thirties, said she was embarrassed. She'd spent years working, raising children, dealing with life. She was glad she was here now. A young man with locks followed. He introduced himself and shared that he'd played too many video games in high school. It was an addiction. He once spent an entire year at home, unable to leave. He would rarely eat or shower. It took several years of therapy to unglue his hands from a game controller. This test, this class, was his new beginning.

It took everything in me, but I stood up and waved. My legs trembled, and it felt as if my knees would buckle. I could feel my heart hammering against my throat. "I'm Vanessa," I said. "I was suspended a few times in school because I'd get into a lot of fights. I was so embarrassed that one day I never returned. I've attempted to take the GED a few times. I've failed again and again. But I hear your eighth time is the charm."

Around me people laughed and cheered. The instructor walked toward me, placed her hand on my shoulder. "I'm so glad you're here," she said.

She handed out registration forms. Feeling empowered, I took one. I filled it out even though the test was in the middle of the day, the same day as the holiday photos at work.

IN THE AFTERNOON Junie came home sulking. The kids hadn't stopped calling her Dark Vader, even though she'd told her teachers. She said it'd gotten worse because even the dark-skinned kids had joined in, and during recess someone had pointed at her hair and said her curls, shrunken and bunched up from her winter hat, looked like Darth Vader's helmet.

"Can I see him again?" Junie asked.

"Darth Vader?"

"Yes."

"Why?"

"Just because," she said. She stood on the tips of her toes and craned her neck upward. "Pretty please."

I googled Darth Vader on my phone and showed it to her. She held the phone close to her face, zooming in on the image.

"I do not look like him," she said, her voice cracking. "What does he do?"

I thought about it for a second. "He's a villain."

"Can I watch a video?"

"Nope," I said. "That's enough Darth Vader for the day."

I got a pack of dinosaur-shaped chicken nuggets out of the freezer and shook some of them into a pan. I texted Mateo, *They haven't stopped calling her Dark Vader.*

Tell your mom. You're not Junie's parent.

It's not that I thought I was Junie's parent; Mateo knew that. He knew what Junie meant to me.

Are you busy? I asked.

I don't really have time to talk right now, he wrote. I tried to convince myself that maybe he was in the middle of something. Regardless, his response stung. I'd made time for him yesterday, even though it wasn't Thursday.

Well, that sucks. I really needed someone to talk to.

I put my phone on Do Not Disturb, then slid it back in my pocket. I wasn't asking for much. I didn't even get to tell him I registered for the GED and would need to leave work early to take the test.

I looked over at the pan. The brontosaurus looked golden. The T. rex on the right needed more time. Chicken nuggets alone weren't enough for dinner, so I grabbed more broccoli. It needed to be eaten.

Junie stared at me from the kitchen table. "Can you cook the broccoli?"

I moved the T. rex over, then placed a handful of broccoli in the pan. The meal looked pitiful. She deserved broccoli that, at the very least, was properly seasoned. She deserved real chicken! Not leftover cartilage and fat, compressed and molded into the shape of an extinct animal. She deserved better. I did too.

THE DAY OF the photo, I arrived at work forty minutes early. I'd been getting there early since Mateo gave me the job, but now that the office had hired a handful of peppy interns with eager dispositions and the willingness to work for free, arriving fifteen minutes early was no longer enough.

Around nine o'clock, people began to trickle in, filling the space with light chatter. I sat in my cubicle— headphones on—listening to an audio file I had just transcribed. Laurie had assigned it to me because the file was in "that Caribbean Spanish." She had wrinkled her mouth when she said this. It made me blink twice.

As I sat there double-checking my work, I saw Laurie approach, Venti cup in her right hand.

"I'm done with that transcription," I said.

"Okay-great-thanks!" said Laurie, almost breathless, each word colliding into the next. "I want to talk to you about something, actually," she added.

I straightened my back and removed my headphones.

"So we're taking the pictures at noon," Laurie began. She placed the cup on my desk, then leaned in. "So for the picture we just want to make sure we look super-duper professional from top to bottom, you know? Not just our clothes but also our makeup and hair, you know?" This she punctuated with a nod, as if prompting me to nod. So I nodded, having understood her subtext.

"We're gonna have to lean really close to make sure we all fit in the frame. Just need to make sure nothing blocks anyone's face. We're going to send these pictures out as holiday cards. Isn't that neat?"

I nodded again, forcing a smile. Laurie grabbed her coffee and pivoted to Yesenia's desk. The only other girl whose curls resembled mine. I watched from my desk, registering the tilt of Laurie's head, the way her head moved up and down like a bobblehead on a car dashboard. Every movement was rehearsed. There was nothing authentic about her pretend concern, no output of genuine emotion. I walked over to Mateo's office and knocked on his door. He looked up from his desk, frowning.

"I think Laurie just asked me to switch up my hair," I said.

"Close the door," he said. "Listen, I'm sure that's not what she meant."

I sneered. "You don't even know what she said."

He sighed and rolled his eyes.

"Unless you *do* know what she said to me." He went back to whatever he was doing without saying another word.

I WALKED TO the nearest pharmacy and picked up a pack of hair ties, a small tub of gel, and a brush. I was the Dark Vader at work. No matter how fast or accurately I typed, or how well I code-switched, I was made to feel indebted to Mateo for the life raft he'd thrown my way.

I approached the register and placed my things onto the counter. The cashier picked up the tub of gel and turned it over to read the ingredients.

"Is it good?" she asked.

"I'm not sure." It was a "strong hold" no-name-brand hair gel for less than three dollars. It couldn't be great. "I just need it to fix my hair real quick," I added.

"Oh, but your hair looks great," she said. And it did. I'd deep conditioned it this morning. I'd used a diffuser to make sure my curls were defined.

"Can I use your bathroom?" I asked.

"Sure. All the way down aisle nine, to the left."

In the bathroom I thought of texting my mother. What would she do? But there was no point in doing so. I wasn't good enough for her. I wasn't good enough at work.

I wetted my hair and parted it in the middle. I squeezed gel onto my palm, then smeared the sticky product on my hair. Within seconds, I felt naked. My hair was supposed to frame my face. I dabbed a bit of lipstick on, then straightened the collar of my button-up shirt. I thanked the cashier on the way out.

Back at the office, a couple of interns were setting up the backdrop for the staff holiday photograph, hanging garlands and Christmas lights and placing gift-wrapped pots overflowing with poinsettias. Mateo stood across the room, smiling that vacant, mechanical smile. Like most days, he didn't look in my direction.

I touched my now slicked hair and thought of Junie. This morning she'd asked for pigtails. She also wanted to forgo wearing her winter hat. How long until she ran out of deep breaths? How long until she started balling up her fists? The more I thought about her, the less I cared about the holiday photo, or about Mateo, or about my mother, or the GED. Junie was, and had always been, the one thing I felt good about. The one thing that made my world feel right. I stopped by my desk and grabbed my purse. I walked toward the elevator and leaned against a cement column, watching as Laurie and the photographer rearranged everyone. People pivoted and turned their bodies sideways. Some were moved to the front, others to the back. Yesenia, now wearing her hair in a bun, and anyone with a tan were strategically peppered throughout the group. Mariah Carey's "All I Want for Christmas Is You" blared from a set of speakers. Mateo stepped out from his position and swiveled his head from left to right. I pressed the down button for the elevator and waited. Right as I heard the ding of the elevator, Mateo locked eyes with me. He patted the front pocket of his suit jacket, followed by the pockets of his slacks, as if searching for his phone. I didn't think he would actually text me. And he never did.

Downstairs, I removed my lanyard and threw it in the trash can next to the exit. I pushed through the revolving doors. Frigid air struck me, so I folded my arms and walked faster, heading toward Junie's school. It was lunchtime, and Junie's teachers would be standing in the courtyard, watching the children play, trying to make sure they kept their coats on. I knew they weren't ready for me. But I was ready for them.

Thirty Miles West

DANNY SPENDS MOST OF SPANISH CLASS THINKING ABOUT
how his dad can't get hard. Last week, when Danny was
at his girlfriend's and they were home alone, he couldn't
get hard either. They were in her room talking about her
mom—whom she hasn't seen in months—when Desiree
began crying. Danny had dabbed her face with his sleeve
and pulled her closer to him. In a fit of emotion, she slid
her cold hand inside his pants. As much as he wanted
to, he couldn't get past her tears and the sad air circulat-
ing between them. He sat there motionless, wondering
if he was destined to be like his father.

From the corner of his eye, Danny sees Mrs. Santiago get up from her desk. When she grabs her clipboard
and starts to walk around the classroom, Danny flips
to the next page in his notebook and pretends to copy
the vocabulary words written on the board. Even if he
wanted to make an effort, he wouldn't be able to. He
can't stop thinking about his dad.

His father is on the upswing, though lately the ups
and downs look very similar. Around 3 a.m., Danny had
woken up to the smell of bacon traveling through the

vents. Mike was sprawled across his bed in his room next door, one sockless foot hanging off the edge. Though Mike is younger, he's taller than Danny, and unusually muscular for someone whose favorite physical activity is thumbing up and down on his phone. Danny reached for Mike's foot, but Mike pulled it away. "I can smell it," he said. On their way to the kitchen, they walked by their parents' room. Their mom was sitting on the bed, her arms crossed, knees folded.

She waved them in. "Close the door," she whispered, patting her bed. Mike sat next to her and pulled her in for a hug. Her small frame fit perfectly inside his arms, like a Russian nesting doll. Danny sat on the edge of the bed and listened to her muffled sobbing.

"It's already bad enough that we're back on this street," she said. "Now we have to be the loud people, the weird people who cook bacon at three in the morning." Most days Danny forgets just how small his mom is. This morning, wrapped in Mike's arms, she had looked even smaller than normal. Exhausted. Danny should have told her then that his dad was skipping his meds.

The ping of Mrs. Santiago's timer jolts him out of his trance. He raises his hand and asks for permission to go to the bathroom. Mrs. Santiago shakes her head and points at the clock. Only five minutes left. Around him everyone is working quietly, so he goes back to his notebook where he's done nothing but draw stick figures of his family.

Danny has known his dad's been skipping his meds for some time now. Before they had to move back to

Newark, before the incident, his dad had told him. "I can't get hard on the fucking meds," he'd said out of nowhere. Danny had looked down at the dirt caked in the soles of his dad's shoes. They had been sitting out on the deck at the old house in the suburbs. It was the middle of the day. His dad had skipped work, and Danny had skipped school. It wasn't the first time they'd both gotten dressed only to turn back around midmorning and find each other at home, blowing off life and responsibilities.

When the bell rings, Danny runs toward Desiree's classroom. This school is not like his old high school in the suburbs. Here the hallways are narrow, and he has to zigzag through foot traffic to make it to his classes on time. There's a way to move around in Newark. Though he spent the last three years in the suburbs, he hasn't forgotten. There is a beat, a tempo. And it's a fast one.

Danny sees Desiree make a sharp left at the stairwell, her big curls bouncing up and down as they get caught in a draft of wind. He reaches for his cell phone to text her, but one of the security guards is posted at the landing of the stairs. The guard, a short man with a belly hanging over his belt, swivels his head left and right, monitoring a trail of students as they run to class.

Desiree texts to tell him they have a sub next period and that he shouldn't bother coming to class. She says to wait for her near the auditorium. Danny wonders if that means they'll be able to be alone. He's never had a girlfriend before. He's messed around with girls at parties and once in a car, but it was different then. He was four-teen and fifteen. That was two years ago, before he was also put on meds.

Instead of going to art class, he and Desiree leave the building. They roll up a school newspaper and stick it underneath one of the back doors to prop it open for when they return. They take Broadway and walk past the White Castle and the McDonald's, and the Dominican restaurant where Danny's mom worked before she went back to college to finish her degree. The degree that made leaving Newark possible in the first place. They stop in front of the restaurant, waiting for the light to turn green. Danny takes in the scent of maduros, empanadas, and chicharrón. Foods they couldn't find in the suburbs and his mom was too busy to make.

When Danny and his family moved back to Newark, they returned to the old place where Danny had grown up. An average multifamily house in front of an empty lot. And now they are renting, again, the second-floor apartment. Most days it feels like they never left. But some days it hurts. Those are the days it feels like they rolled the dice and landed on a square that says "Go back to the start."

North Newark is beautiful in the spring. Though the wind has blown some of the flowers away, cherry blossom trees are in full bloom. Their branches curve downward, forming umbrellas. A bed of petals cush-ions the sidewalk like pink snow. At the deli, Desiree orders Taylor ham, egg, and cheese on a bagel while Danny stares at her face—the brown of her skin, the few freckles that dot the bridge of her nose. Because of all the bacon he ate, he only gets an apple juice.

They alternate between streets with modest homes (like the one his family lives in), homes like Desiree's (which look like they're on the verge of collapsing), and million-dollar mansions hiding behind tall fences surrounding the perimeter, protected by alarms and dogs—remnants of the Newark old white people reminisce about.

On a bench near the tennis courts, they watch a flock of commuters heading to the light-rail station. They remind Danny of times when he and Mike would walk near the tracks, hoping to intercept their dad on his mail route so he would get them Italian ices from the Rita's down the street.

Desiree takes a huge bite of her bagel; grease drips down her chin. "Yes, Danny?" she says when she catches him staring. "Can I help you?"

"You can kiss me," he says.

She leans forward and opens her mouth—full of chewed-up food—and a tendril of steam rises into the air. "It's so hot," she mumbles.

"So no kiss?"

"Maybe later. How's your dad?" she asks. Danny doesn't know how to answer the question, or maybe he just doesn't want to, so he says nothing.

They waste another ten minutes at the park before heading back to school. She kisses him before they sneak back into the building, a long wet kiss that makes his heart beat faster. Still, nothing happens below the waist.

He wraps his arms around her and kisses the side of her face. "Okay, now," she says, so he lets go and they both head inside.

WHEN DANNY AND his family moved out of Newark, it felt as if they'd crossed a finish line. It was a different world, just thirty miles west. There were no sidewalks in their town and they had to drive everywhere, but they had a garden where they grew strawberries and tomatoes, where they spotted deer and even an occasional bear. They had a yard and a driveway. His dad was happy and talked about building a pool one day. Mike's asthma didn't flare up anymore, and his mom acted like she had just won the lottery, like she had been literally handed her American dream.

What Danny didn't know was how a foreign place would suck the life out of him. Like a harness too tight around his chest, squeezing the air out of his lungs. He likes to think that it was the quiet that drove him insane, the dewy, noiseless morning air, and not his father's genetic code.

Before the night he lost it, Danny hadn't known he had it in him. He was wired from winning a wrestling match, a sport he had claimed he would never compete in. But there he was, feeling larger than life, drinking beer in Peter's basement. He and the rest of the team were throwing darts at a wall and pretending to keep score when Peter came downstairs cradling a cigar box. They followed him and sat in a circle on an old carpet that smelled faintly of Peter's dog. An Ariana Grande song played in the background. "What the fuck is this girly shit?" Peter shouted, turning it off. There, right before the game started, Danny knew he should have gone home.

When Peter lifted the lid of the cigar box, Danny was confused. For a brief moment Danny had thought they would smoke, or take some pills, or maybe even snort something. Instead Peter took out a revolver. Somebody called his name, but it got drowned out in the noise that followed. Danny had never seen a gun in real life. Sure, people in Newark got shot all the time. But no one he knew owned a gun.

"Russian roulette," said Peter, before pointing the gun at Danny's head and pulling the trigger. Danny felt as if his heart stopped at the click of the empty barrel. After the click, the last thing he heard was someone yelling, "It's not even loaded!" Then came the laughter. It erupted out of Peter and out of everyone else. Laughter, the guttural, knee-slapping kind. It reverberated and lingered even after Danny'd grabbed the gun and hit the side of Peter's head with it. Danny could still hear the laughter as he pummeled through Peter's eye socket and into his skull. And for as long as he heard it, he couldn't stop himself.

WHEN DANNY ARRIVES late to AP Composition, Ms. Morini gets up from her desk to open the door for him. She only opens it slightly and peeks her head out. "Mr. Rodriguez," she begins. "Do you have a late pass?" Danny shakes his head, and she continues to stare at him. She steps out and folds her arms, stretching out her foot to keep the door from closing behind her. "This is not how we do things here." She tucks her long brown hair behind her ear. She's young and tries really hard to sound firm, and it works because no one here *actually* wants trouble. Danny wants to tell her she can break character; she can breathe. Instead he says, "Yes, ma'am," and lowers his head as he walks in.

Danny gets a text message from his father. Because his father is still on the upswing, he wants to pick up Danny and Mike from school right after fourth period. It doesn't matter that neither Mike nor Danny wants to leave. He texts them saying, *I'm outside.* Danny grabs his backpack and puts it on his desk to make it easier to hide his phone from his teacher. *That's not how this works*, he texts back. *You need to come inside and properly sign us out.*

Jesus, his dad responds. *Life is too short. Live a little.*

Danny meets Mike in front of the auditorium, where they sneak out through an emergency exit. Neither one of them says a word. They walk side by side and look at each other. This has happened before. Their dad gets an idea, a breath of spontaneity, and they follow along.

Their dad waits for them in the car at the corner. He's parked right in front of the fire hydrant, his caution lights flashing. "I thought you had work, Dad," Mike says. Their dad doesn't say anything.

Danny feels his cell phone vibrate in his pocket once again. It's Mike. He puts it on silent so their dad doesn't notice they're texting each other behind his back.

Bruh, he's still wearing his uniform, Mike texts.

Danny gets in the front seat of the car. "¿Por qué el uniforme?" he asks his dad.

His dad gives him a once-over, smiling. "When you bring out the Spanish, I feel like I'm in trouble!" He puts his arms around Danny's shoulders. "Don't worry about it," he says. "Let's just have a good day, please."

When Danny or his dad are about to cry, they blink a mile a minute. They tilt their heads back, as if telling the oncoming tears to stop dead in their tracks. Most days they succeed, but only for so long before an outburst of emotion explodes out of nowhere.

In the car, their dad plays Rush. He taps a beat on the steering wheel and headbangs to the tune. He says, "Who's the drummer, Danny?" Danny looks at Mike, hoping he'll chime in, but Mike's head is leaning against the window and his eyes are closed. Danny's sure he's pretending to be asleep. "Come on, Danny," his dad insists. He is smiling so wide Danny can see the empty space where a tooth used to be. "Who's on the drums? C'mon! You know this. You know who this is."

Danny tells him he doesn't know. Truth is, he barely even knows the band. Danny turns around to look at Mike, who is now on his phone. His father looks at his hands and sees that Danny is also holding his phone. He honks the horn, causing other drivers to honk their horns too. "Is it just impossible for youse guys to just let loose for a goddamn minute?"

Danny wants to ask him what's going on, but sometimes it's best to stay quiet. The night of the incident, after his father came to the station and the police released Danny, they sat in the car without saying a word. Several days would pass before his dad insisted on talking about it. At night he would sit on Danny's bed and place a hand on his back, filling the emptiness around Danny with his presence.

An hour into the drive, their dad tells them they're going to Asbury Park for a stroll on the boardwalk. His breathing is steady. He is smiling again.

Once in Asbury, he loops around looking for free parking. They drive in circles for what seems like an eternity. Danny points out open parking spots while Mike keeps his head buried in his phone. "We got a winner," their dad says when he finally finds a spot they fit into. He squeezes in and demands that they all leave their phones in the car. For a brief moment everything is still. Danny can hear the waves crashing. He can almost taste the saltiness of the air.

On the boardwalk they stop at the first hot-dog stand they see. Their dad orders for them, then grabs the ketchup and squirts it onto Danny's shirt. "Pew pew," he says, fashioning his hands like a gun before running off toward the water. Mike stares at the glob of ketchup on Danny's shirt. His head swivels as he scans their surroundings, his face a hot red.

Danny grabs the ketchup bottle and points it at Mike. "Don't even think about it," Mike says. Danny puts it back down.

"You're always entertaining his bullshit," Mike adds.

"What am I supposed to do?"

"I don't know, dude," Mike says. "Maybe not make him feel like this is okay."

When Mike talks like this, Danny wants to pound his face until his cheekbones crack and crumble under his fist. He would sock him right this second if he knew he could stop himself.

"You don't know what it's like," Danny says.

Off in the distance, their father kicks off his shoes. In front of the water, he looks like a statue: two feet planted firmly in the cold sand, unbothered by the undertow. His arms are spread wide, as if waiting for an embrace, for someone or something to hold him, to give him something he needs. Danny watches him soak up the sun, thinking how, right now, at this very moment, his father seems happy.

They return to the car and find the window on the left-hand passenger side broken. Their backpacks, phones, and sweaters are missing. The red Solo cup where their dad keeps loose change has been turned upside down. Old CDs lie scattered about, some of them cracked and snapped in half, as if whoever broke into the car had a personal grievance against their dad's music choices.

Mike screams "Fuck!" over and over. He holds his head with both hands and kicks one of the tires repeatedly before he walks away. When Danny goes to chase after him, his dad holds his arm.

"Just let him," he says.

When Mike makes it back to the car, Danny asks him if he wants to sit in the front. "There's no fucking way I want to sit next to that man." He says it loud enough for their dad to hear him. He gets in the back, takes a deep breath, and rests his head against the window.

Danny watches the speeding traffic flicker past them. Everything moves so fast. Without his phone, it's hard to keep his eyes open. He closes his eyes and thinks of Desiree. He's sure she's heard about the incident, though he personally hasn't told her about that night, about the court dates and the mandated therapy and the fact that they lost their home to lawyer fees, or the sad reality that Peter will never be able to see from his left eye again. About the rage he feels surging inside him from time to time.

Out of nowhere, his dad takes an exit so recklessly that the tires screech on the pavement and their bodies jerk forward. His gaze shifts from one mirror to the other. He merges into the left lane, then turns off the radio. "I'm just trying to get us home fast," he says.

A woman in a small red car flips them off, mouthing curse words. Some cars speed past them while others slow down. Everyone's trying to get out of their way. His dad lets go of the steering wheel to wipe sweat off his forehead. The honking of angry drivers makes Danny wish he'd told his mom about the meds.

Mike yells, "Stop the fucking car!" But their dad doesn't stop. "Stop the car, you fucking psycho," he screams, reaching for the wheel. Danny pushes Mike's hand out the way, and their dad slams on the brakes.

"What the fuck are you doing?" Danny asks as Mike is thrown out of his seat, nearly hitting the dashboard.

The car behind them stops short of rear-ending them.

On the opposite side of the highway, drivers rubberneck in their direction. Danny's looking for the Budweiser brewery, a landmark that tells him they're almost home. He doesn't see it. His mother's little Dominican flag hanging from the rearview mirror swings like a pendulum, and the clock on the radio blinks 12:00 repeatedly. Neither his dad nor his mom has fixed it.

Their dad merges and pulls over on the shoulder. Silence spreads. When Danny closes his eyes, he's reminded of a time when a trip to the arcade took the three of them across state lines. North Newark became Delaware, Delaware became Virginia, and then green farmland too beautiful to be home stretched before them. One day blurred into the next as his dad cycled through every CD in the car. Bachata and rap and classic rock—the mixed bag of genres he loves. He and Mike sang along, hopeful, fearful, and anxious to be home before the joy that propelled this adventure ran its course.

"Enough," Danny says.

He squeezes right above his dad's kneecap. "Hand me the keys." His voice is firm and unwavering. He waits with an open palm until his dad hands them over.

After they switch sides, Danny readjusts the seat and counts to five, each steady breath slowing time until he feels ready to drive home. He turns his head and watches his dad lean back, take off his work shoes, and put his feet up on the dashboard. Veins, large and twisted like the roots of an old tree, crowd the tight skin of his father's calves. Purple lumps trail from the back of his knee to his ankle. They give Danny pause.

He notices how his father's shoulders rise and fall, how his pulsating jaw unclenches, how his rigid face softens. The more Danny stares at him, the more he understands he's looking at a man different from himself.

The World as We Know It

THE FIRST NIGHT JOY AND I HEARD THE THUD, WE DIDN'T know what to make of it. We were lying in bed and Joy was applying that anti-wrinkle cream she bought after one of her students told her white people age faster, while I scrolled through Reddit posts about Trump building a wall. The government was experiencing the longest consecutive shutdown in history, and much like the government, I was getting shut down by Joy every night. Nighttime showers followed by the tiniest drop of Armani cologne didn't do the trick; neither did the thorough manscaping I was doing for her. Nor did the push-ups, pull-ups, or flossing. For three weeks Trump had been attempting to get funding for this unnecessary wall while I tried to romance my girlfriend, both to no avail.

It seemed like everywhere I turned, the wall was all anyone talked about. From my parents—middle-aged, self-described moderate conservatives from Livingston—who believed we needed it to stop the alien invasion threatening to obliterate the world as we knew it, to Joy, who thought we breathed too much air, took up too much space, and shamelessly basked in our whiteness, treading mud and leaving the sticky foot-print of our privilege wherever we went.

So as I scrolled down a barrage of racist comments, I shook my head in silence and kept them to myself. Getting Joy fired up about politics would always lead to this cycle of misery where she would write letters to our representatives and post Facebook updates about the apocalyptic state of our government. This would lead to virtual fights with friends, family, and every covert racist on NJ.com. I would complain about her zealotry, and we would end up fighting and not having sex. It was as if, once started, Joy would tug at that frayed thread of our relationship until everything came undone.

When the thud became a bang, Joy looked at me, doe eyed. She walked toward the vent and stood on the tips of her toes, her calves flexing, beautiful and toned—the product of five-mile daily runs—trying to listen for noises that were no longer happening.

"It's not coming from upstairs," I said, putting down my phone.

She looked at me like I didn't know what I was talking about.

"I'm pretty sure it's Mark and Sabrina," she said.

Mark and Sabrina were new to the three-unit walk-up where we lived and, like us, they were white and relatively new to the city. When Joy attempted to give them tips for how to survive in Newark—once the murder capital of the United States—they practically told her to fuck off. At least that's how Joy interpreted their encounter.

"It's definitely them," she insisted. "They're probably drunk or high, doing who knows what."

It bothered Joy that Mark and Sabrina felt as comfortable as the locals. They never seemed to worry about strolling down Pacific or Adams late at night wearing expensive jewelry and using their expensive phones. Often enough they would leave their backpacks out on the front seat of their car, a 2018 Honda Civic, which, to add insult to injury, they often left unlocked. It was as if all the worries that unsettled Joy didn't apply to them. She had this theory that maybe they felt at ease because they didn't look as white as us. Mark's hair was dark and curly, and he transformed into this golden statue after just a few hours in the sun. Sabrina's lips were full, her hips round, and her ass, well, I don't know, maybe it looked ethnic. But it was none of our business, which I reiterated to Joy.

It wasn't that Newark was particularly hostile to us. The Ironbound was pleasant. It was just that we didn't fit in. Though the Ironbound was quite diverse, white people were outnumbered, or underrepresented, however you want to put it. On any given day you could encounter over a dozen different nationalities easily, though not the generic white Americans (like Joy and me) that everyone loved to hate. There just weren't that many of us. And the few of us who did live here were considered gentrifiers.

After standing by the silent vent for an additional minute, Joy let out a defeated "whatever" and jumped back into bed. When I turned to face her, my eyes landed on her nipples. They were hard and pointy, so I made a move, straddling her and kissing her neck. I aimed for her lips, but she switched off the lamp and turned her face away from me.

"Can't you take a hint?" she said.

"There are nicer ways to say no."

"No means no, Eddie."

"You didn't even say no," I said.

"But did you hear me say 'yes'?"

I began to lose my erection. In the darkness of the room, I could no longer see Joy's face, but I imagined her disdainful expression. I kept quiet, as if to let her know I had no desire for a petty argument this late on a school night.

THE NEXT DAY at lunch, I walked over to Joy's classroom. Her door was open and she was standing at the whiteboard working with Marquise, Danny, and Desiree. I knocked gently. "Coming out to lunch?" I said, car keys in hand. She looked at me, then turned back to the board.

"Ayo, Mr. B, we're busy," said Marquise, getting up from his desk to shake my hand.

I pointed at a list of SAT vocab words written on the board. "Man, you know that stuff," I said. "I taught you that last year."

"Not well enough, obviously," said Joy.

In unison, all three kids yelled "Burn!" Their exaggerated laughter echoed through the room. Marquise slapped his knees; Danny and Desiree high-fived each other. Then they all high-fived Joy. I smiled and watched her smile, too, deep lines forming at the corners of her mouth, eyes glimmering with warmth.

"Okay, now, it wasn't *that* funny," I said, still smiling.

"You're just big mad because Ms. Morini is a better teacher."

Joy looked at me and winked, and I stuck my tongue out at her, enjoying the momentary truce. "I might be hanging out with these guys after school," she said.

For the third week in a row, Joy was hosting a tutoring session during lunch. We hadn't eaten lunch together in nearly a month. She was tutoring after school as well, and she would come home late and insist on going on a run alone. At night she didn't want to watch TV or cook together. Over the weekends she held more tutoring sessions, drove kids to and from practice, and volunteered at the recreational center. All things that didn't include me.

Later that evening I hesitated before putting on my sneakers and heading out for a run. Without Joy, running seemed useless, even painful. I wasn't sure why the fuck I ran in the first place; it was Joy's thing. I hated getting looked at. I hated being that white guy looping the neighborhood aimlessly. I also hated the burning in my calves, the throbbing in my Achilles tendons, the sweat dripping down my back. But I went anyway.

After a couple of circles around Independence Park, I walked slowly toward the soccer field. Standing on the outskirts, I watched a few Mexicans kick a ball back and forth. On any evening where the temperature was above forty degrees, and the breeze was gentle and the moon was bright, you'd normally see dozens of people playing sports in the park. But not this evening. As a matter of fact, lately crowds seemed sparse. Everything looked emptier. There were fewer cars on the streets, fewer people double-parking during street-cleaning days, fewer kids smoking. Something in the air felt different.

At home I resolved to tell Joy that her attitude sucked, that we hadn't had sex in three weeks or talked about anything other than politics, and I was unhappy. But that loud thud returned, disrupting my plans. This time I agreed to step out into the hallway.

I thought I recognized the voices of Miranda and Julio, our downstairs neighbors, and their five-year-old son, Gabriel, speaking words beyond the scope of my shitty high school Spanish. First Julio's voice—stern, angry. Then Miranda screamed something that sounded like "Stop!" The last thing I heard was Gabriel crying. I ran up and down the stairs, stomping my feet as loudly as I could, hoping the sound would alert them to my presence and make them stop. Their voices became whispers, and I waited a couple minutes before taking another step.

Miranda and Julio were normally quiet people. We didn't know much about them, other than that they were Dominican immigrants. Joy had guessed this based on their darker skin and Caribbean Spanish. In the mornings Julio would get picked up by a crew of local construction workers, and he often returned home late at night, covered in a thick film of dust. Miranda often smelled like Pine-Sol and bleach. Their English was limited, so we never had long conversations.

I tiptoed back upstairs to our apartment, where Joy was standing on the welcome mat with her arms folded. Her pink shorts were riding up, exposing her inner-thigh birthmark. She stood there, squared up as if ready to tackle something. Her long brown hair was flipped to the side, tousled and beautiful.

"You could have locked yourself out," she said.

"I know. Pretty sure it was Miranda and Julio, by the way."

She paused. "They seemed so nice."

I rolled my eyes. She was always so quick to write people off. "Well, this doesn't mean they're not nice," I said.

She huffed, tiny droplets of spit spraying the air around her. "Sounds like they're beating their child."

"We don't know that," I said.

"Really now?" She looked at me with disdain.

"Really now?" I repeated. It was hard to remember that there was a time when our words were not peppered with sarcasm. A time when we made love, watched mindless TV, drank beer, and ate pizza. A time when we couldn't bear the thought of holding on to anger.

Joy turned around and made her way to the bedroom. I spent the night on the couch.

I FELL IN love with Joy when we were in college. The day I noticed how beautiful she was, one frigid January morning, I was walking to class with my hands in my pockets. Joy wore blue jeans and a pair of brown Uggs that matched her coat. Her long hair was tied in a loose bun, bouncing as she walked, because when Joy walked, there was a spring in her step, a little jolt that said she was on to something. She was holding on to this girl—a blind student I often saw on campus—who was walking slowly with her cane.

Joy guided her around, especially during poor conditions like sleet or snow. She would walk with her to class, then pick her up after and accompany her back to her dorm. Later I would come to find out that Joy would clean her room, buy her groceries, and even help her get ready for a date here and there.

As for me, whenever things were broken and needed fixing, Joy was there. When I flunked a semester during our sophomore year of college, it was Joy who threw out all my weed and confiscated my Xbox, who forced me to wake up in the mornings, who made me study.

It was as if anytime I lacked purpose, I could look at her and find it there. After we graduated, when she decided to teach in Newark, I followed.

AT THE CRACK of dawn, Joy's oxford shoes were already hammering on the hardwood floors. Still on the couch, I stretched to grab my phone off the coffee table. It was testing week, and my absence from school wouldn't be felt as much, so I faked a cold and forwarded my sub plans to the department chair.

The scent of Joy's perfume lingered. Right on top of

the hamper in our bathroom was the T-shirt she wore to sleep, black cotton ruined by a fine mist of bleach. Depending on where you sniffed the shirt, it smelled different. Around the neckline you'd get Joy's shampoo, sweet and herbal, and near the armpits you'd get that musky scent of her nighttime sweat. I grabbed it and held it to my face. On TV, a reporter wearing a pale blue blazer said the fight about building the wall was far from over. She and another reporter discussed the implications of the government shutdown, listing possible catastrophes ranging from labor strikes to famine.

Frustrated, I figured I would jerk off and go back to sleep, but the moment I put my hand on my dick, a loud pounding startled me. There just wasn't a moment of fucking peace in this place. I got off the couch and ran down the stairs. Miranda stood in the foyer. She waved her hands at me frantically. Her mouth was moving fast, spewing something so jumbled that it resembled neither English nor Spanish. I did recognize one word: "Help."

I looked through the peephole and saw two middle-aged white women. They wore frumpy clothes and sensible shoes and held clipboards like the social workers at school. I looked at Miranda and waved her away. When Miranda went back inside her apartment, I opened the door leading outside the building and introduced myself to the visitors, caseworkers from Child Protective Services, who said they'd received a call regarding the welfare of a child who lived in one of the units. I knew immediately that this was about Miranda's son, Gabriel. And also about Joy.

I cleared my throat and assured the women it must have been a mistake. The one wearing a green cardigan asked if I knew why someone would request a visit. She leaned against the door, reasserting her presence. I rubbed my arms for warmth. "I can't think of any reason why someone would call you," I said. "I'm a teacher. I would have noticed something unusual or alarming." They both looked at me and then, as if choreographed, thanked me before handing me their contact info. I watched as they walked to a gray Toyota parked right outside. They sat in their cars and waited a few minutes before driving away.

Miranda came out of her apartment. Her cheeks were streaked with dark blotches of red. She thanked me and clasped my hands. Her palms were slick with sweat. Something about her eyes—this softness, I guess—made her look vulnerable and afraid.

That evening Joy came home tired as usual. After I told her she'd made a terrible mistake, she looked at me and said, "I don't think so. I mean, you heard all the noises too." I had heard the noises, but Miranda and Julio just didn't seem like the kind of people who would physically abuse their kid. And the kid never seemed unhappy or injured to me.

"What about respecting their culture?" I asked. "You sure it's okay to interfere?"

She averted her gaze. "Sure. But this is clearly different," she said, then trailed off to the bedroom. I followed her, but she slammed the door in my face. "At least I know I can sleep at night," she said.

It was hard to accept that this was who we had become. We owed nothing to the world, or to this city, or to these people.

I stared at a framed photograph on our bookshelf, of Joy holding two shovels next to a snowman we'd just built. We were so grateful for the foot of snow that kept us home for a few days. That week we played Connect Four, Scrabble, and Dance Central on the Xbox. We made love on the gray three-seater couch we had just bought from IKEA—now deformed by a faint outline of my body.

For the second night in a row I slept on the couch. I called out of work again. I knew at this point I would probably be asked to provide some sort of excuse for missing two days in a row, but I just didn't care. The thought of seeing Joy at school made my stomach churn with anxiety.

Around six in the morning she came out of the bedroom, stomping her feet as loudly as she could. As she left she looked in my direction and mumbled "dick" under her breath.

Later that morning the TV reporter with the funny blazers said Trump and Congress had reached an impasse during a fourteen-minute meeting with Democratic congressional leaders. Someone mentioned the possibility of using disaster-relief funding to pay for the wall.

Across the country TSA agents were going hungry. Volunteers were running soup kitchens to feed government workers who hadn't been paid for weeks. I watched a news segment where reporters took to the streets, asking random passersby to weigh in on the issue. A bunch of different folks agreed that the shutdown was devastating. I wondered if the chaotic state of our country churned inside of Joy's head twenty-four seven.

The wall was changing us. It was changing life around us. The Ironbound, an immigrant haven, was starting to feel different. People seemed on edge, as if they knew they had to watch their backs. On Facebook, a buddy of mine described how a suspicious-looking van (with suspicious-looking white people) parked for a bit too long at the corner of South and Jefferson, and like an apocalyptic game of telephone, a rumor began that the van was an undercover ICE vehicle conducting an operation. People in the area believed there was a deportation raid in the works, so they ran for their lives.

Fear permeated everything. Even the soft-spoken lady who worked at the bodega near our place had vanished. One day she was there, and the next she was gone. A tall younger woman who spoke English fluently had taken her place.

I drank a six-pack of beer and went on Pornhub, purposely looking for all the ethnic porn a man could watch in a day, which is a lot of porn.

I searched for Latinas and Asians and Black girls (or "Ebony")—all of these marginalized women Joy spent all of her time talking about. Somehow I wanted to fuck all of them. I pulled down my basketball shorts and masturbated on the couch, secretly hoping Joy would walk in on me and drown me in one of her speeches. After finishing up, I wiped off my belly button with Joy's bedtime T-shirt and leaned my head on the armrest.

I reached for my phone and noticed a text from her. *You should be here*, it said.

I texted back, *It's not that big a deal.*

It's annoying that everyone keeps asking about you.

Tell them I'm sick. I wanted to get off the phone, but she was still typing.

I'm not your keeper, Eddie.

But you are my girlfriend, I texted. I stared at my screen, waiting for the blinking dots to turn into words.

This is why we shouldn't teach at the same school.

I paused, not knowing how to reply.

Maybe there's a lot we shouldn't do, she added.

I wanted to ask, *Why don't you love me anymore?* Instead I put my phone down and closed my eyes.

I WAS DRIFTING into restless sleep when a loud knock on the main entrance door jolted me awake. This couldn't be fucking happening again. I waited a little, thinking perhaps I was delirious and imagining the noise, but it grew louder.

I got up and walked into the hallway, still drunk from the six-pack. As I began to descend the staircase, I heard a "shhh" and a gasp, and then the sound of feet scurrying about. At the front door, two officers wearing blue ICE vests were speaking to Sabrina, asking for a Miranda and a Julio Gonzalez. A routine check-in, they said.

"May I please come in, ma'am?" asked the older officer, whose fitted polo seemed to be strangling his biceps. Sabrina, still holding on to a dishrag, stepped to the side.

Sabrina teared up. Perhaps seeing those ICE agents

hit close to home. Perhaps she knew something about Julio and Miranda that I didn't know. I couldn't fathom her agony. I didn't know what to say to her. I imagined Julio's and Miranda's lives would never be the same. I watched from the periphery, realizing I had left the TV on.

The reporters were at it again, several voices interrupting one another. The government was still experiencing the longest consecutive shutdown in history as the political parties debated that fucking wall. As the officers knocked on Miranda and Julio's door, all I could think about was Joy feeling guilty and ashamed, unable to eat or sleep. The ICE agents grew tired of knocking. They slipped a letter under the door and left. Sabrina walked over to Miranda and Julio's door and said that it was safe to come out. No one did.

The world as they knew it was over.

I walked back inside our apartment and thought of calling Joy, of asking her to come home as soon as possible. But I felt paralyzed. Heat spread on my forehead and breathing became difficult.

I waited on the couch until she came home. She set her keys on the table and looked at me. For a moment I couldn't even form the words.

"ICE came for Miranda and Julio," I managed.

She stood there. "What do you mean?"

"My guess is CPS contacted someone. I don't even know."

She looked confused, as if the gravity of what I'd just said hadn't registered. "Do you think it's serious?"

"It's ICE, Joy."

Her eyes welled up, and she went from looking sad to looking sick. She ran to the bathroom. Her long hair draped over the toilet bowl. I grabbed her arms and helped her stand up.

"Did I do this?" she asked. "Is this my fault?"

She walked back to the living room and paced back and forth, stopping only to press her face against our door, as if trying to listen for something.

"What if we get them a lawyer? What if we call your dad?" she asked.

"I don't know, Joy. I don't know how any of this works." The bitter taste in my mouth overwhelmed me. There was nothing left to do.

"Please hold me," Joy said. When it became clear that I didn't feel like touching her, she reached for my waist and pulled down my shorts. On her knees, she proceeded to suck my dick, tears mixed in with her saliva. I didn't stop her.

Once she finished me off, I helped lift her up and urged her to go to bed. She tossed, turned, and cried most of the night, and told me repeatedly that she didn't mean to. That she would find a way to fix it.

Sometime before the sun came up, I heard Miranda, Julio, and their son leaving. We never saw them again. Over the next few days, strangers would enter and exit their apartment, carrying out boxes and furniture. Joy had trouble sleeping. She'd slip her cold hands inside my shirt, and I would hold my breath in silence.

JOY AND I sat at our small kitchen table and watched airplanes fly over our street. Some flew high enough that their hum was barely audible; some flew so low they cast shadows that dimmed the room. The shutdown was over, though the uneasiness remained.

When we first moved into the apartment, we played this stupid game where we would take turns guessing which airline the plane flying past our window belonged to. Living so close to the airport sucked, but we loved this game. Perhaps because we were in love with the novelty of our lives here: the airplanes, the neighborhood, the students with all their warmth and inappropriate senses of humor.

Joy picked at some stir-fried vegetables I had whipped up for dinner, cutting the veggies into smaller pieces and rearranging them on the plate. I stood by the kitchen counter and took a good look around me. The plants near the window above the sink were dying. I couldn't remember for the life of me when either of us had last watered them. Fruit flies hovered near a couple of wrinkled lemons covered in white fuzz.

"Do you want to go for a walk?" I asked. "Or maybe grab something else to eat? This food sucks."

She shrugged, then said, "Okay."

On the sidewalk, I held her hand. It sat limply on my palm for a few seconds before I let it go. Just a year ago, she had joked about keeping her nails manicured in case I finally decided to propose. But she never did. I wished I could put my finger on the very moment when everything changed. The moment when Joy stopped making those jokes and I stopped thinking about proposing.

We walked down Barbara and Wilson. From there we strolled down Ferry, past the coffee shops with outdoor seating and the old Portuguese men drinking espressos and smoking cigarettes. They laughed and blabbered in what sounded faintly like Spanish, punctuated by "shhh" noises at the end of some words. We smiled politely as we walked through their clouds of smoke, Joy's elegant frame speeding up ahead of me, gracefully swaying.

At the Brazilian café the server attempted to take our order in English. Usually in this neighborhood people assumed you spoke their native language, and you had to try to make sense of it. We watched her struggle, remaining patient.

"They're accommodating us," Joy whispered as I took a sip of water. "You don't think so?"

"I don't think what?"

"You don't think they're trying to accommodate us? They probably feel pressure to speak English, you know."

I wanted to say, "Not today." Instead I asked if that was a bad thing.

"It's a sad thing," she said.

We ordered a little bit of everything: mozzarella sticks, coxinhas, pão de queijo. We ate some of it in silence. When the server approached us, I smiled and nodded awkwardly. The food was fine. We just weren't all that hungry.

The server came back with a box. She thanked us and handed over the check. I overtipped, without Joy's prodding—she always tipped extra everywhere we went in the neighborhood, as if we were paying an additional tax for breathing air that didn't belong to us.

On our walk back home, Joy lowered her gaze and picked at a hangnail on her index finger. I took hold of her hand once again and traced her knuckles, registering how it felt to touch her skin. Perhaps I was stupid for thinking our world would end with a cataclysmic event. Though maybe I knew all along that it would come down to the little things. The little frictions that start off earthquakes.

Bear Hunting Season

THE PROBLEM WAS THAT NINA'S HUSBAND WAS DEAD. In the year since his passing, she had joined a support group of widows. Women who, despite having suffered unimaginable loss, were learning to cope by knitting, baking, running in the park, learning tae kwon do, or passing around Joan Didion's book about grief like a safety blanket. Older women who insisted she was young enough to start over.

The women spoke about themselves as if they were in recovery and grief was a substance they could wean themselves off if they tried hard enough. Perhaps because Jeremy's death was still fairly recent, or because she wasn't even thirty years old, Nina couldn't imagine ever feeling anything other than gut-wrenching despair. Nothing sparked optimism. Not even her youth. If anything, it made her feel inadequate and defenseless, like a baby lurching down a steep set of stairs without a banister to hold on to.

Like most nights, that Tuesday she woke up gasping for air and writhing out from under two weighted blankets like a snake shedding its skin. She wrapped her right hand around her wrist until her fingers left indentations.

She then squeezed each of her arms, then her shoulders, and the nape of her neck. No one had touched her in months. Not her family, not her friends, not strangers trying to make their way through a crowded Penn Station. She felt a kind of emotional and physical void that made her bones ache, made her wonder what it even felt like to have someone else's fingers pressed against her flesh—anyone's.

She rolled over and grabbed her phone off the nightstand. She couldn't quell the late-night panic attacks, so she planned to scroll on Instagram until her eyes glazed over. She thumbed up and down until she noticed a post from Claudia, one of the widows from her grief group. Nina zoomed in on the photo of Claudia and a man she had met through LoveAgain, a dating app designed exclusively for widows and widowers. Claudia, who had only worn black since her husband passed, had a green sweater on. The bright shade suited her, as did her new haircut. The picture made Nina smile in a way she hadn't expected. It was as if Claudia had removed her cloak of grief, revealing a new, healed version of herself. Nina lingered on the photo and wondered if that could ever be her. What would it be like to start over?

A few months ago, at the widows' insistence, she had made an account. Now she searched for the app's logo on her phone, a pair of mourning doves perched on a branch, beaks touching. "Mourning doves?" she said out loud, looking at the image. She rolled her eyes, then googled doves, scrolling deeper into a rabbit hole of meaningless trivia. She learned that doves were supposedly monogamous, but then read this wasn't unique to doves as most birds mate for life.

She believed she would have spent the rest of her life with Jeremy. They had begun dating when she was twenty-one. They shared a world of firsts: first apartment, first car, first vacation, first promotion. But now Jeremy was gone, and she was reading about doves—mourning doves—and it reminded her of that Prince song, so she stopped her search to play the song, then wondered if doves actually cried. Was Prince referring to the tremolo of their cooing, or did he mean actual tears? Which she came to find was indeed a possibility because doves had tear ducts that kept their eyes from drying out. But were the tears always functional, or could they also be the byproduct of grief, of sadness? She realized she was crying, like she had every day for the past year—in paroxysms that would appear out of nowhere, as unpredictable as hiccups.

She wiped her face, then browsed for a photo of herself to include in her dating profile, eventually deciding against every picture. She no longer looked the same. Her husband had died only a year ago, but her face now seemed unrecognizable. She had lost weight, and her cheeks were hollowed. Her smile looked too wide for her now small face. If she were to do this, she needed to be honest. No catfishing. So she sat up on the bed, flipped her hair to the side, and held her phone up to the light. She snapped a selfie and looked at it, zooming in on her eyes, noticing how even her eyelashes looked thinner in the gaps between clumps from days-old mascara.

She tried to scoot over to the left side of the bed—her husband's side—where a tall brass lamp curved overhead, but there were objects strewn all over: a bottle of lotion, hand sanitizer, the case for her glasses, a cellphone charger, a notebook, a handful of pens. This pile of things took up more space than the husband himself had. She pushed them over and onto the floor, unflinchingly waiting for the noise to stop.

Under the more flattering light, she snapped the photo and deemed it good enough to post. It occurred to her, once she put her phone down, that she had lost track of her late husband's urn—or rather, the wooden box where she kept the few spoonfuls of ashes she had left. The box, usually next to her in bed, was no longer there. Had she pushed it off the bed with everything else? Had she thrown it away somehow? What if the ashes were now scattered all over her trash?

She took a deep breath. There was no way she could have accidentally disposed of her husband like that. Not when she'd been carrying his remains with her for nearly a year.

She found the box on her nightstand. Relieved, she hugged it, held it tightly to her chest, then put it down on her lap and opened it. She paused for a moment, asking herself in disbelief if she would do *that thing* again. She unfolded the small plastic bag inside the box and then slipped her fingers into it, massaging the ashes against the tips of her fingers like grains of sand. Then she licked her fingers, gagging at the strange but comforting taste, and at the thought of her sickness—the compulsion she'd succumbed to after her body demanded what remained of him, like a sort of latent nutrient deficiency. She closed the box and set it next to her on the bed.

She turned her attention back to her phone. The dating app unsettled her. It made her feel watched, an animal behind tempered glass. Regardless, she went ahead and made a profile, self-identifying as a widow.

It hadn't been an hour when she received a message. A white man from somewhere in the middle of New Jersey, a town she didn't recognize. In his profile photo he wore a blue hat and a polo shirt. Sitting on a bench at a boardwalk, he balanced a marlin on his lap as he smiled from ear to ear. He seemed attractive in an older, modest way. He hadn't specified his age, but based on the photo, she assumed he was in his forties.

He wrote, *Hello, how are you? I wish this didn't feel so awkward.*

The greeting, unthreatening and unpretentious, endeared him to her. *It's awkward, but it's okay*, she responded.

They chatted back and forth, talking about the app, the pros and cons of dating fellow widows and widowers, the risk of wallowing in twice the amount of grief, of basking in unchecked sorrow. But addicts, he told her, befriend one another all the time despite their perpetual urges. Maybe they could become friends who helped one another stave off grief, or at least kept it from multiplying.

His name was Henry, and he said it would be best if she didn't ask about his wife. The request brought her a sense of relief because she couldn't talk about her husband, or about the freak accident and the way she had been living in squalor and isolation since then, which hadn't been helped by her recently becoming unemployed.

When he suggested they meet, she agreed almost immediately. She looked hazily at the screen, squinting at his photo. Maybe Henry would bring an interlude to her sadness, a pause long enough for her to unlearn her panicked breathing, the loud gasps for air that blindsided her at random hours of the day.

Henry said he could drive out to Newark. His grandmother, a Polish immigrant, had grown up in the Ironbound. When he was a kid, his family would buy kielbasa from a Polish butcher, a man who knew the family from the old country and would speak to them in Polish despite being completely fluent in English. She didn't have the heart to tell him that the deli had closed years ago, the inside of the store gutted and turned into an unlikely boutique. Instead she let him message with deep nostalgia for a place he hadn't visited in years. *Do you like kielbasa?* he asked, then suggested they pick some up and take it to his cabin in rural Jersey. He could grill it for her, and he had a fantastic wine that'd pair nicely. He had so much of it he didn't know what to do with it. Kielbasa or otherwise, he'd make her anything she'd like.

A home-cooked meal, much like physical touch, was something she craved. When was the last time she had a fresh home-cooked meal? Not a casserole delivered to her doorstep, made with equal parts pity and morbid curiosity for the woman whose husband choked to death a few feet away from her. A husband who, in his pursuit of air, had knocked down the wedding photos on their credenza as he grabbed a chair from the dining set and attempted to give himself the Heimlich maneuver. Who had, in his dying breath—or lack thereof—dialed 911 after learning, presumably, that he wouldn't make it to the basement where his wife, wearing noise-canceling headphones, cardioed her fat away on a treadmill machine he had never agreed on buying in the first place. Every casserole came with questions, with the presumption that she would talk about her husband's death and answer the preternatural "*how.*" *How could you let this happen? How could you not hear any of it?*

THEY MET ON the sidewalk across from the site of the old deli. Cigarette in hand, Henry waved Nina over. Nina stood paralyzed, speechless at the sight of this stranger, at her failure to let him know the old deli was now a boutique.

She walked over to him and attempted to shake his hand. "Nina," she said with a quavering voice, as if she were borrowing her name, usurping a person she no longer was. She moved closer, registering his brown eyes. A tiny skin tag dangled from the corner of his eyelid like a teardrop made of flesh. His long brown hair spilled from the sides of a loose bun. Still, he was attractive in the way he stood confidently, tall, his broad shoulders unapologetically taking up space.

Henry smiled. "I don't like to shake hands," he said. He flicked the tip of his cigarette and took a last drag before putting it out on the heel of his boot. He was much taller than Nina. "That doesn't offend you, right? Also, we already kind of know each other," he added.

It didn't offend her. To feel something, even the slightest indignation, would take more energy than she had at the moment.

"Yeah, no, it's fine," she said. She stared down at her shoes, a pair of black boots scuffed at the toes. An old Christmas present from her husband. She asked him for a cigarette, though she had never smoked a day in her life.

Henry pulled a pack of American Spirits from his back pocket. He took out a cigarette, but he put it in his mouth instead of handing it over. "You don't smoke," he said.

"How do you know?"

He chuckled. "You have the nicest smile I've ever seen. Also, you'd have your own cigarettes if you did." He took out another cigarette and handed it to Nina. She took the cigarette and placed it between her middle and index fingers.

She'd grown up in a household of heavy smokers. Her husband had been one himself until she'd demanded he quit, though she knew he'd never completely stop. She had once seen him outside his job sneaking a cigarette. "You'd at least have your own lighter," he added.

Nina looked at him and nodded, unsure how to respond. She'd come to dread conversations since her husband died. She always felt uncomfortable around other people. His untimely, unusual death both canonized him and vilified her, making it so that no one in her immediate circle wanted to speak to her. Her brother and sister-in-law no longer talked to her. And she had been avoiding her mother, fearing she'd judge her for allowing something like this to happen. She hadn't caused her husband's death, yet everyone acted like she had. She felt their judgment on her skin, in the way their lingering gazes lasered through her. How could she have let this happen? Other widows had had no choice. Their spouses had succumbed to ailments and circumstances fully beyond their control.

She caught herself staring at Henry's body, his perfect posture. The sudden realization that she was in his presence made her palms sweat.

"Grab a drink with me," he said, breaking the awkward silence brewing between them. "It's obvious we're not buying any meat today." He winked in what seemed like an attempt to ease her anxiety over the kielbasa faux pas.

She tried to think of a bar to take him to, a quiet place where they could talk. She considered her apartment but quickly disregarded the idea when she remembered she'd knocked over the pile of things taking up half the bed. They still sat on the floor, probably aggravating the ant problem she'd been having.

"Let's go to the cigar bar," he said before she could offer a suggestion. "Since we both smoke." He winked again.

It surprised her that he seemed to know his way around the city. She wiped her sweaty hands on her jeans. "I'm sorry about the deli," she said.

"Oh, please. I already knew."

The fact that he hadn't told her he already knew and met her there anyway seemed duplicitous, weird, even. But maybe he was simply treading lightly, trying to ward off any seedling of discomfort. Perhaps he was trying to be nice because he, too, understood how weird it was for her to come out to meet him, this strange man who wasn't her husband.

THE CIGAR BAR was nestled between the arena and the train station. It was more of a speakeasy, a local gem of sorts, known for live music and hand-rolled Cubans. It had a corporate clientele on some days, an artistic one on others.

Henry led the way through a sloped parking lot and a paved patio encircled by vines and dangling lights. In the center, a fountain spouted water from a statue of a Greek goddess. Patrons sat around metal bistro tables with their drinks. Women in black dresses walked around cutting and lighting cigars for men in suits— beautiful, young, thin women who all looked the same from a distance.

Nina remembered that her husband had frequented this place. She imagined, nonsensically, that she would turn a corner and find him smoking there, talking to one of the servers. But there was no husband to run into.

He was dead, his presence a projection of her faulty memory.

Henry glided through clusters of people, jauntily stopping now and then to greet someone. It was fascinating to watch him; it seemed as if everyone knew him and as if he knew everyone. With his rugged looks and his confidence, Nina couldn't imagine him as a grieving widower sitting at a support group with other widowers.

The cigar bar had once been someone's house. Inside there was a living room with dim lighting, leather couches, tables, bookshelves, and a grandfather clock. A jazz singer stood in the corner, riffing off the crowd. There was another bar out back where another server made craft cocktails with bitters and tinctures.

He asked her if she wanted an old-fashioned. She nodded. When he handed it to her, his hand brushed against hers. "What do you miss most?" he whispered in her ear.

The question made Nina pause. Not because she hadn't thought about it before, but rather because the question was always there, like the low hum of the air-conditioning.

"What do I miss most?" she repeated.

"Yes."

She didn't know where to begin. Nothing seemed to belong to her anymore. Not the apartment she had shared with her husband or the places they'd frequented, not even her own body. Every aspect of her being was tethered to a memory.

"I miss everything, I think." She wondered how long it would be until she told him she carried her husband's ashes everywhere she went. That in moments when she couldn't hush the howl of grief, she ate them until her stomach lurched in protest.

Henry looked at her. "You don't," he said. "You miss you. You just gotta find you."

He spoke with the authority of someone who had mastered grief. Nina wondered if that was part of the future that awaited her once she crossed the finish line—the imaginary threshold of sorrow, the frontier that divided joy from pain.

He told her she needed to "burn the oil of her suffering." Since his wife had died, he had become a hunter. He hunted pheasants, ducks, deer, and bears, he told her, and in doing so he exerted control over *life*, over another being's existence. It helped excise his grief, halt its machinations.

"Come with me," he said. "Let's hunt a bear."

She laughed unexpectedly. "I could never."

"Why not?"

"Because it isn't me."

"We can do anything you'd like to do. May I?" he asked before tucking her hair behind her ear, a gesture that made her feel tender. Maybe he was right, she thought. Maybe what she needed was to sit in stillness.

"What would we even do with a dead bear?" she asked.

"Turn it into a rug," he said. "Just imagine sitting on it, bare-legged and barefooted, running your hands through its plush coat." He reached for her face, then ran his fingers across her cheeks. Soft, softer. She'd been harboring the suspicion that maybe Henry didn't like her all that much. But the gentleness of his touch made her feel otherwise. It was a tender and disarming gesture that made her yearn for more—that made her feel like she was a person, not just a widow.

She imagined the rug, and she imagined herself wielding a gun, in charge of her life the way Henry seemed to be in charge of his. It was enough to make her wonder if she was ready for an unexpected thrill. A jolt that would make her feel like time was moving again.

NINA TOOK A week to think about it. She had never hunted before. She'd never even held a gun, so shooting a bear was out of the question. She had seen a black bear once roaming near the hiking trails, then running away as soon as it caught sight of humans. But the thought of killing one had never occurred to her. Her husband hadn't hunted. He was the kind of man who'd ushered bugs to safety, cupping his gentle hands around each intruder and returning it to its element outside their home.

She'd read about bear hunting season in the paper, but she'd chalked it up to a thing white people did out of boredom. A woman like her had no reason to harm a bear, let alone hunt it for sport. But maybe this was what healing was, an exploration of the unknown, an excavation of soil that doesn't belong to you.

Nina had no idea where to even begin with hunting,

so it was up to Henry to handle the logistics. He let her borrow a camouflage sweatshirt, which she wore with a dark pair of leggings. It wasn't the best hunting outfit, but as there were only a few days left of bear hunting season, he didn't think Nina needed to spend money on hunting clothes she may only ever wear once. He also let her borrow a hat and asked her to tie her hair up to keep it away from her face. She would be there and observe, act as a companion, not as a hunter herself. He would make sure he executed the kill shot. Afterward, if everything worked according to plan, he would call a friend to help them move the bear onto Henry's property. In response to all of this, Nina remained optimistic, excited even, to be a part of it.

Henry had already been stalking the bear, a midsize male that he said had meandered onto his property twice already, eating his shrubs and brambles with abandon. They camped out behind a large tree near the bend of a creek for the bear to come out.

During the long stretches of silence, Henry ran his fingers across her palm, carefully caressing her wrists, then leaned in for a silent kiss on the side of her face. In the woods, amid the burbles of the creek, she could hear nothing but her own gentle breathing, the quiet inhale, exhale she'd been controlling to keep her pulse steady. It seemed as if she'd explode at the slightest touch from his hands.

A couple of hours into the hunt, they spotted the bear: large, then larger as he got closer. Nina hadn't predicted how seeing the animal's body would make her feel. The bear's presence, though unintrusive, rattled her insides. The bear seemed almost majestic. Innocent in the way that it moved about, unaware that it was now prey and not predator. Nina watched as it ambled near the creek. Its looming death now seemed unfair. An aberration, much like her husband's.

Her heart beat faster with each of the bear's crunching steps. She could feel the palpitations in her throat, the pulse of her heart at her temples. Fearing that the bear might hear it too, she held her breath and watched as Henry nodded and drew his rifle, preparing for what looked like a clear shot. She thought the anticipation might kill her. She pulled a pair of silicone earplugs from her right pocket and slowly pushed them into her ears, wishing to avoid not the boom of the rifle but rather whatever noise would come out of the dying bear's mouth—maybe something like the sounds her husband must have made gasping for air, trying to dislodge the hard candy stuck in his throat.

A few minutes had passed and Henry hadn't taken the shot. Nina began to dread it. Would it suffer? How long would it take for it to die, to stop feeling pain, for its brain to stop firing nerve impulses, like electric currents traveling through live wire?

Henry continued to stand perfectly still. His focus made Nina increasingly aware of her own uneasiness. Her legs felt restless, and the more she tried to keep them still, the more she felt them cramping up. Anxious, she inadvertently stepped on a branch, the snap loud enough to alert the bear. Henry, still aiming, took his shot as the bear ran. But he missed it by a few inches. He lowered the rifle, then dropped to his knees, his face tinged with a look of defeat. He looked at Nina, then wiped his brow and took a deep breath.

"I'm sorry," Nina said. He didn't respond. He picked up his rifle and then turned around. Nina, ashamed of her mistake, followed.

"I'm not upset," he said. "I just need a moment."

He stopped, crouched, and sat on the ground, bending forward to hang his head between his knees. Nina didn't know what to offer other than apologies for having ruined the hunt. Henry would now either have to travel outside the state or wait a year for the next hunting season. The idea made Nina anxious. She felt guilty and responsible. If this was his coping mechanism, what would he do until then? What would mollify his sadness, bring him some reprieve?

Henry extended his hand as if asking her to help pull him up. But when she grabbed his hand, he pulled her down onto him. She fell on top of his body and froze, paralyzed and unsure what to make of the gesture. But then he hugged her, embraced her so tightly her bones crunched a little, and she felt something akin to comfort and relief. She smiled at him, and he smiled back, reassuring her he wasn't angry. One thing he had, he told her, was time. The next bear hunting season would come, and if he was lucky enough, she would be there.

IN THE CABIN, he cooked her a steak, rare, though she asked for medium. She imagined he had slaughtered the cow, butchered it into consumable bits, boiled the bones and marrow until they disintegrated and congealed, cured its skin and turned it into leather. He poured her a glass of wine. The bubbles reminded her of gurgling blood. She thought of the bear, how they weren't able to kill it. She wondered whether it was still out there, roaming, waiting.

Henry raised his glass. "Salud."

"Salud," she responded, her eyes fixed on the mantelpiece. She hadn't noticed it before, but there it was, on top of the mantelpiece, a picture of Henry and his wife—a curly-haired woman with round wide hips like hers. She felt a pang of sadness for the dead wife who reminded her of herself. Then she felt a gnawing, a feeling she couldn't quite place.

She ate in silence, trying to ignore the heaviness of the dead woman's sudden presence. She tried to focus on the meal. The steak he cooked. The salad he made. And when that wasn't enough, she tried to focus on Henry. The way he touched her. The patience and grace he continued to show her.

After dinner, she moved to the couch, where Henry kept refilling her wine glass. He pulled her toward him, which made her smile; then he kissed her. She kissed him back, and it felt like she was dipping her feet into a pool, waiting to get used to the temperature—awkward at first, until she found her pace and rhythm. After a moment he grabbed her hand and led her toward his bed.

Henry was comforting, indisputably so. He enveloped her body, and while he held her, he seemed to become a bear himself—large and warm. He kissed her as he brushed her hair behind her ears, holding her face with his left hand. He pressed his body against her, biting her bottom lip, breathing hurriedly into her ear. He cupped her breasts and pulled at her nipples, and when she moaned, he pulled a little harder, twisting with his forefinger and thumb until her moan morphed into little yelps of pleasure and pain. She slid her hand inside his pants, stroking him gently. But then he went soft under her hand. She stopped and removed her hand from his pants. Wanting to disappear, she avoided his gaze.

"I'm sorry. I'm so sorry," he said, still on top of her.

She wanted to say "It happens," but it'd never happened with any man she'd slept with before, at least not in her presence, and so she began to wonder if she had done something wrong to spoil the moment. Did he not find her attractive enough? Was she too desperate or too sad or too weird?

Before she could utter a word, she felt a droplet land on her cheek. Henry, suddenly smaller, was crying. "I have something to tell you," he began. "I haven't been able to, you know, since my wife died."

"Able to have sex? We don't need to have sex," she said.

"Able to stay hard."

She couldn't quite understand what that was like. But she empathized with him, reiterating that they could do anything else instead, that she felt the best she'd felt in a year.

He sat on the bed, legs crossed. "I need to hold something of hers," he said. "I'm embarrassed to say it's the only thing that works for me these days."

She thought of the people she'd met at the support group. She had learned they all kept reliquaries. They'd all held on to something sacred from their former lives. Some women still texted their husbands. Some listened to voicemail greetings on repeat. Some slept next to their dead loved one's clothes. He was speaking to her in a language she understood.

With a glance, a wordless plea, he gestured at a pile of folded clothes sitting on top of his dresser. "Would you? Just this once." She considered the request and the silence that would follow after she obliged *this one time* for the sake of his emotional release. She grabbed a pair of his wife's leggings off the dresser. She held them in the air while looking at him as if to ask, *Are you sure?* And when he nodded, she slipped each of her legs in, pulling the leggings up toward her navel, tugging here and there to adjust the fit. The leggings clung to her body like a second skin, as if they belonged to her, as if he had planned this all along. That sudden thought felt almost disembodied. However, it didn't matter. She would wear the clothes and extend this moment of grace, however strange the act might feel, because she wished someone would do it for her.

She grabbed the tank top. The scent of the dead wife's perfume rose into the air, overwhelming her for a moment. She looked at his yearning face but instead saw her own, imagining the way she cradled that box and swirled her late husband's ashes with her fingers. She couldn't fathom a whisper of judgment, for either him or herself, so she slipped the shirt on and smoothed out its creases, watching as Henry wiped his tears and waved her to climb onto the bed.

She kissed his forehead and furrowed brow. She sat up and cradled his head on her chest, letting him sob himself to sleep. Hours would go by before she'd slip out of the dead woman's clothes. Before she would walk to the brook. Before she would, finally, scatter her husband's ashes, wailing as if trying to keep the bears away.

What Is Yours

THE FIRST TIME I THOUGHT ABOUT KILLING JEFFREY, WE were sitting in front of a white backdrop, holding our breaths and wearing matching embroidered shirts flaunting a last name that felt like gumballs inside my mouth. Mom wasn't Jeffrey's wife, and I wasn't Jeffrey's kid.

I sat between them as instructed by the Sears employee posing as a photographer. Jeffrey's big palm lingered on my thigh, and the heat emanating from it made the skin under my jeans hot with shame. He lifted his hand to his mouth. With his tongue, bumpy, thick, and seemingly swollen, he licked all four fingers, but since he didn't gather enough spit, he licked them again. A faint string of saliva stretched from his mouth to his hand, and before I could swat it away, the hand reached my head and forcibly flattened the curly strays that rebelled against the humid July air.

"I thought I gave you enough money to get the girl's hair done," he said to Mom through gritted teeth. She continued to look straight ahead, forcing a wider grin— the scar on her face folded into her cheek like a dimple curving along her smile lines.

Mom had done my hair that morning, struggling as she had for all sixteen years of my life. Without keeping in touch with my father or his family, she never learned how to style my hair. She would try but become flustered and eventually give up. During most of elementary school, she'd forget to comb my curls, and they would knot. My hair would get so matted either Mom or Jeffrey would shave it and then throw a girly headband on my head as if that could make up for it. I never knew whose idea it was, but they both did it from time to time, as it was easier to manage a shaved head than kinky curls.

With the money Jeffrey gave her, Mom bought herself name-brand foundation and concealer to mask her scar. The once-deep reds against the pale white of her skin had somewhat faded over time. The gash itself seemed smaller, but the marks left by the stitches, all five of them—sewn unevenly by Jeffrey's hands—still rose like little welts.

It was the stitches, not the gash itself, that made people look twice. They told the real story. They were Jeffrey's way of marking his territory, as deliberately as an animal pissing on a patch of dirt it wished to call its own.

JEFFREY'S GIRLS WERE pretty and broken in all the right places. I heard once, by eavesdropping on my mom and a neighbor, that before Mom, there was a beautiful woman with a sharp nose, big striking brown eyes, and a mouthful of rotten teeth. Another girl he picked up from Willa's was supposedly just as beautiful, but she had an alcohol problem and an abusive ex-husband. Then along came Mom with a gash on her face and a crack habit and a mixed-race kid who looked nothing like her. Jeffrey was that bargain shopper who only took home discarded pieces from the clearance rack. He had a good eye for all the pretty things with stains, rips, snags, and holes.

The day Jeffrey found us, we were outside Willa's Tavern, wedged between two dumpsters; I was seven and she was twenty-three. With one hand Mom held her cheek, split open by a knife wound that came from a petty confrontation with a drug dealer; with the other she held on to me. A mixture of blood and tears streamed down her chin as she bellowed on the ground, and I cried too—because of her nails sinking into my wrist, and the thundering bass that seeped out from Willa's, and the fluorescent streetlamps in the parking lot, and the gravel denting my skin, and the whirlwind of confusion that stirred around us. I cried because I saw Jeffrey's face and I saw his eyes, and he didn't frown, and he didn't gasp, and he didn't speak softly, and he didn't say much. He just ushered us into his beat-up F-150 and drove us to his house.

As we sat in Sears for our family portrait, it wasn't just my hair reverting to its natural form that ruined the moment; it was also that white backdrop highlighting the brown of my skin, shouting that not only was I not his, but I never could have been his in the first place. Against that blank canvas I was more colorful than ever—unwillingly defying their whiteness, reminding Jeffrey we couldn't fool the world; I was mine. We were nothing but a quilt that came from patching up all the wrong that could exist in one place.

On the way back home, I rested my head against the car window and imagined what it would be like if I reached for the steering wheel and turned it toward the median. I could see us spinning, flipping, dying. Maybe Mom and I would make it out. We were young.

Mom looked back at me. "There's a lighter inside my purse," she said, with a cigarette in her mouth.

"You're gonna get that nasty smell all over our clothes," I said.

She extended her hand toward me, a web of blue veins protruding from her pale white skin. I folded my arms and looked the other way. Jeffrey looked at me, frowning, and said, "Give your mom what she asked for."

I handed her the lighter. She lit up her cigarette, then squeezed Jeffrey's thigh. I thought maybe that night I would slit his throat.

IN THE FALL I thought about killing Jeffrey almost every night. I thought about greasing the tub right before he showered. I imagined he would slip and fall, hitting the back of his head. Mom would be too high to hear a thing, and I would ignore his cry for help. I imagined I would crush one of Mom's pills and mix it into his Cutty Sark. I imagined I would shoot him with that hunting rifle he kept in the shed.

Once, over dinner, he choked on a mouthful of chewy beef chunks. He coughed uncontrollably, spit splattering all over the place, and I felt a rush creep up inside me as his face began to turn blue. Mom ran to him. "Don't just fucking sit there!" But I wanted to just sit there. I wanted to know, if he dropped dead then and there, would Mom just be better? Could we just be better?

Though I couldn't conjure a plan or think concretely about his death, I knew that for Mom to be free, Jeffrey needed to be gone. But instead of figuring out the details, I watched the oak out front bare itself naked, leaving our windows exposed. The leaves fell harder that fall, in indiscriminate large numbers, first imperceptibly and then not.

Mom upgraded to heroin. Everything around us changed. She stopped getting arrested on drug charges, and people now referred to her problem as an illness, a disease, a crisis all over New Jersey. White people were shooting up. White people were smoking crack. White people were dying. Governor Christie said it was an epidemic, like AIDS. I couldn't tell the difference.

That fall we didn't see Mom often. She would come home to fuck Jeffrey, to delude him into believing our lives could be different. She didn't bother with me.

JEFFREY WAS ON his third glass of Cutty Sark when he said we needed to clean out the gutters. He took the last swig and looked at me. "Better now than later," he said.

The leaves had been accumulating since late August. Compounded by the mixture of rain and dirt, they hardened and stuck to the gutters like concrete. I grabbed the ladder from the shed and brought it to the front of the old house like Jeffrey instructed. Though we didn't take good care of the house, a one-story shack that had belonged to his late mother, we did just enough to keep it from falling apart. Mom never helped. It was always Jeffrey and me fixing what we could.

The house sat right at the border of North Newark and Belleville, just a few yards from the projects. Nestled between Branch Brook Park and the local hospital, it was one of those few homes that managed to stay occupied by its original owner during white flight. Like its surroundings, the foundation of the house was barely keeping it together.

Inside the house there was mildew just about everywhere, and the smell of cigarettes permeated almost every surface. When the old woman lived here, the place reeked of disease. A waft of urine, feces, and smoke would smack you right at the door. Once she passed and we moved from the basement to the first floor, not much changed. We replaced one sick old woman with a junkie who could only stay clean for weeks at a time.

When she was clean, Mom would play the role of wife well enough to appease Jeffrey, but never long enough to fool me. She would clean and cook and shop for pretty house things—a vase here, some knickknacks there, a plant that would die shortly after. She would hug me occasionally and even ask about my day, trying to bridge the distance that had widened between us since my birth.

Keeping Jeffrey satisfied didn't take much though. He was perpetually lonely, perpetually hungry, perpetually trying to anchor himself to justify his pitiful existence.

He was at least twenty years her senior, an awkward and lanky white man with a speech impediment—always the butt of cruel jokes about inbreeding.

He needed Mom to make him feel like a man, and she needed him to help her survive. She made him feel wanted the way men want to feel wanted, I guessed. With the thin Sheetrock walls that separated my room from theirs, it was impossible not to hear them have sex. Mom made exaggerated noises even I knew had to be fake while Jeffrey grunted and moaned.

I propped the ladder against the side of the house and waited. Jeffrey walked toward me, blocking the sunlight with one hand. He paused right in front of me and stared. His staring always had this way of making me feel naked and ashamed, as if he was examining my worth.

"We waited too long to do this," I said.

"Well, whose fault is that?"

"Mine, I guess."

As my luck would have it, anything that went wrong—which was everything, if you asked me—was my fault. Mom and Jeffrey never failed to remind me. He looked at me as if carefully choosing his words. I already knew the litany that would follow: a reminder about how lucky I was to live in his home, to wear clean clothes to school, to eat three meals a day, to have a family. Other girls like me—other Black girls, he would say—didn't have it so good. I could be sucking dick on the street. And he was right; things could have been much worse. It could have been me sucking his dick instead of my mother.

Jeffrey stood at the bottom of the ladder, holding it as I climbed each step. I told him I'd made sure it was steady, but he insisted on offering additional support. As I dug into the gutters, scooping up gunk with my hand, his presence clouded the air around me. He stood just inches below my body, watching me work. I imagined him on the ladder instead. I imagined I would kick the ladder with my foot, or maybe I would let go of it right when both of his arms were reaching up, or maybe I would just push him and watch him fall on his back. Maybe at the hospital I would place a pillow over his head and watch him squirm as he struggled to breathe.

I scooped up wet leaves and even the semblance of a dead bird, long decomposed. I dumped it all onto a trash bag that sat open on a patch of grass below. Jeffrey continued to watch me, unbothered by the bits of dirty water that splashed his way. He lingered like he always did, reminding me of my place in his world.

THE ONLY TIME Mom asked if Jeffrey had ever touched me, she paused to answer her own question. "You know what, never mind," she said. "He doesn't like Black people." She followed this with a chuckle and a drag of her cigarette.

"Do you like Black people?" I asked. "You liked my father enough to make me." I somewhat expected her to turn away in outrage. But she didn't. She paused and looked at me with those big brown eyes that seemed to apologize to everyone but me.

"I like *you*," she said.

I never asked again. I wanted to say, *How can you hate what is yours?* But we lived at the intersection where love and hate converged. Had we been able to choose one of the two, our lives would have been easier.

IN THE WINTER I stopped fantasizing about Jeffrey's death. All I could think about was potential energy: the inherent energy an object possesses based on its position relative to other objects. If it were me Mom leaned on, if she loved *me* instead, just how different would she be?

The more time Mom spent out of the house, the more I got to take a good look at Jeffrey. Everything he did seemed to leave a footprint of sadness: the way he stood waiting for her to come home, the way he rushed to the front door at the faintest noise, like a dog waiting for its owner. I didn't know where we would be if he were dead. I realized that Mom, for sure, wouldn't be free.

That winter snow was unkind, holding us hostage every week or so. School was canceled often, so I spent a lot of time sitting around at home doing nothing. To my surprise, Jeffrey didn't ask me to shovel as he normally would. He took on the bulk of those tasks himself, pausing every so often to catch his breath. From the window I watched him pile snow into a mound on the front yard and pour extra salt on the walkway to make sure Mom would be safe. Once inside he would ask about my homework, about school, about boys, about life. At times it seemed he cared.

There was no telling what would happen if Jeffrey

were dead. Perhaps nothing would happen if any of us were dead. We would always be a broken vessel. No amount of glue would ever hold us in place.

That same winter Mom disappeared on us for good—a bender that outlasted all of her other benders. Jeffrey would come home and ask about her with a deflated voice. The answer was still the same: She had not come home, and no one had seen her around town. She hadn't been picked up by the police, and she hadn't been in the hospital. Jeffrey was desperate this time, even venturing out to the projects on his own and, in a fit of despair, crying into my arms while we ate pizza on the couch. She was nowhere to be found. Not by the light-rail station or the tracks where people shot up. Not in the abandoned houses of the North Ward or the South Ward or the West.

Near the Davenport Street stop, I asked everyone in sight if they had seen the white lady with the scar on her cheek. I showed them the family photograph we had taken that summer at Sears. A woman with locks stared at my face. "Ain't you Desiree?" she asked. "Ain't you Veronica's daughter?" Her right hand was now grabbing my shoulder. She told me I looked like my mother, and that was the first time I'd heard anyone say such a thing. It was also the first time I'd heard someone say my mother talked about me. Before I left for the next bus stop, the woman told me that she, too, had been wondering about my mom. No one had seen her in weeks.

At night Jeffrey cried himself to sleep. He made howling noises and gasped for air. He sounded like he was dying, and I began to fear his heart would give out.

Right before Christmas break, he picked me up from school. To my surprise, he wanted to talk to one of my teachers. I watched him enter the building. He almost looked like someone else, or like another version of himself. He wore his Levi jeans, but his flannel shirt was tucked in, with a brown belt that matched his boots. His hair was neatly combed to the side.

He smiled and tapped my shoulder. "So where are you taking me?"

On the way to my science classroom, he tripped near the edge of the stairs. My heart jumped at the thought of his body rolling down the steps, his fragile head hitting the concrete.

"Holy shit!" I screamed, holding on to him. I pulled him up and embraced him. "Thank God," I said.

He looked at me and laughed. "You saved my life there."

Inside the classroom, Jeffrey extended his hand to Ms. Guzman. "I'm Desiree's stepdad." I looked at him, noticing the soft smile lines at the corners of his mouth. Then I looked at Ms. Guzman's face, wondering what she was thinking. In over two years of high school, I had never brought in anyone from home. No one ever showed up to a conference. No one ever picked up a report card or even looked at it.

"It's so nice to meet you," she said.

They talked about my grades and my potential. Every so often, Jeffrey would look back at me, his eyes pleading for something.

In the car he played jazz. His fingers tapped the

steering wheel gently. He looped around the park, taking the longest possible route and stopping whenever he saw a crowd of people gathering. I knew that he would never stop looking for her.

I also knew that love was a complicated thing to define. From the looks of it, Jeffrey loved my mother, but I couldn't help but wonder who exactly he loved. I tried to make peace with the notion that there was a different woman somewhere in there, a woman worthy of love, but she wasn't the mother I knew. Like Jeffrey, I was also waiting for her to come home.

I had been waiting all my life.

Jászárokszállás, Hungary, or Newark, New Jersey, or Anywhere, USA

AT SIXTEEN, IT IS THE BOYS FROM JÁSZÁROKSZÁLLÁS, Hungary; a place where they had never seen skin as dark as yours, or hair that spirals and springs like a Slinky.

The boys in Jászárokszállás want to take turns looking at your naked body. They sit on buckets, milking goats and fantasizing about the color of your nipples. They yell "Hey, baby!" amid laughter. Two words they learned from rap songs.

In Lake Balaton, they stare at you while you mindlessly take in the sun. What would happen to your skin if you fell asleep on a cloudless day? They don't know how much light you can absorb, how each ray of sunlight deposits more color.

Then it is the boys at home, and they are curious too. They tell you they'd love to try someone like you. You hear the words "dick-sucking lips" and "fuck-me hair" for the first time.

A boy in Newark, New Jersey, tells you he's Puerto Rican, but he's not. Eminem is his favorite rapper, and he knows how to cook tostones. Those are twice-fried plantains, he explains. In conversation, he drops the N-word, but he says it's okay: He's got a pass from his

Black friends. He just happens to be in a white body. If he had a black dick, he'd be a porn star. He admits he's actually Italian. And even though his skin is so white it is basically translucent, Italians are not white, he insists. And he's dated girls like you. He, in fact, only dates girls *like you.*

You turn twenty and meet a boy in New Paltz, New York. He writes you a letter in Spanish. He needs to practice the pluperfect tense; he also wants to kiss your full lips. He says opposites attract. You write back and wish him success.

In Providence, Rhode Island, a random white boy approaches you just to tell you he's Blacker than you. He knows who Q-Tip is and you don't. He can name all the affiliates of the Wu-Tang Clan. He puts his hand inside your shirt, unclasping your bra. "Have you ever been with a white guy?"

You say, "A couple." You're drunk and curious, but you've come to expect this, so you walk away.

In Littleton, Colorado, there's the one who tells you he's always wanted a Black girl. He says an ass the size of yours has better suction. He can take you out to lunch and even a movie. You can hold hands and date for a while, in his car, in your dorm, in an alleyway between two bars. This one you like, but you will never meet his mom.

You are twenty-six and in Boston when a white man with a septum piercing asks if he can sit next to you. He once dated a Black girl and he didn't like it, but some things you have to try twice before you make up your mind. He has two children but would love one more. Biracial children are beautiful. Obama was a good president, he admits. He tells you he is a Republican. And no, he didn't vote for Trump. He says this country is divided. "Not everything is about race." His white cum would look so lovely against your Black skin. "Do you get easily offended?" and "Can I buy you a drink?" You finish your beer and ask for the check.

In Lafayette, Indiana, it happens again. "Do you know how pretty you are?" some white man asks. "I've never dated outside my race." You smile politely and sit somewhere else. The encounters increase, as does your apathy. The more places you go, the more things are the same.

Then there's an Uber driver in Austin, Texas, and a teacher at the airport in Houston, and a server in Philadelphia, and another in Chattanooga, and a man from Cleveland who washes and seasons his chicken, and you are twenty-seven, and twenty-eight, and twenty-nine. You didn't ask for it then. You're not asking for it now.

Soon you will be thirty and you'll meet a couple back home who will ask for a "swirl threesome," and you'll picture an ice-cream cone and a Sunday morning by the Hudson as you watch the ferry drop off tourists across the river. You'll laugh it off. You know it won't stop. It never does.

There is nothing you can do about it.

The Other Carmen

WE ARE IN THE STUDY ROOM IN THE CAMPUS LIBRARY working on a group project when it happens. Underneath the large conference table, as if I couldn't tell from across the room, Nicole slides her hands inside Evan's pants and begins to stroke him. Before reclining and stretching out his legs, Evan moves his laptop: a lousy divider to give him the illusion of privacy.

I think of Dr. Shrupka and how I wish he were here in the room with us. If he were here, he would see this categorically undeniable evidence that I can disappear before Nicole's eyes. I've brought this up to him before. I even referenced *Invisible Man*. When I asked him if he knew what I was talking about, he nodded and said, "Ralph Ellison, yes." Then he went back to looking the way he does in that big-ass leather chair. I'm not saying Dr. Shrupka doesn't take me seriously when I bring up Nicole. It's just that he sits there motionless, as if waiting for me to say more.

The moment I stand up, Evan's body jerks forward. Nicole looks in my direction and gives me a wink before mouthing "bye." I grab my phone and my bottle of water and head to the bathroom. If being dark and fat can sometimes make me invisible, it's worse when Nicole is around. When I'm not invisible, I'm an afterthought. When I'm not an afterthought, I'm an instrument of self-adulation—the mirror-mirror-on-the-wall reflecting back a flattering version of herself. I've tried to explain to Dr. Shrupka that I only exist to her when she needs an audience. It's worse than not existing at all.

I tell Dr. Shrupka everything, like what I eat and don't eat in a day, or how much I drink and smoke, or how I deliberately choose to ignore my parents' calls. The latter makes him shake his head. But he doesn't say much. At times he'll ask what makes me sad. I tell him I don't know. It's like death by a thousand paper cuts: home, school, family, friends, Nicole, Evan, *Nicole and Evan*, the world. Everything?

I even told him about my latest obsession, which isn't Nicole but rather this porn star who, like me, is named Carmen Diaz. I found the other Carmen by googling myself. When I typed my name in the search bar, I wasn't expecting to get more than a few unflattering photos of myself floating around the Internet. But instead I found Carmen—a porn star who not only had my exact first and last name but also looked so much like me. Her dark skin, wide hips, big breasts, and her fat stomach. It was like looking at myself, but an unapologetic happy version.

In the bathroom I splash water on my face and scroll down Twitter for a few minutes. I take slow breaths the way I imagine the other Carmen does when she feels stressed. I close my eyes and there she is, inhaling and holding in her breath. Her shoulders drop with each exhale and she smiles. Eventually I feel composed enough to return.

The doorknob to the study room feels warm in my cold hands. I turn it a little harder than necessary to give them a few seconds to fix themselves. Evan is standing up, his hands clasped loosely near his zipper. "We missed you," he says. His voice is perky, presumably from the adrenaline. The study room is a mess, like everything has been hastily moved out of the way to make room for fucking.

Nicole and I met Evan during our freshman year of Equal Opportunity Fund, where they teach us poor kids how to get through college. Dark and athletic, with a mouth full of perfect teeth, Evan spoke Spanish and Kreyol, danced bachata, and knew every Dominican dish involving plantains by name. He was funny and had a way of making me feel at ease.

The first time Evan and I kissed, we were at a frat party. It was around four in the morning, and everyone had either left or fallen asleep. I was picking red Solo cups off the floor, because it felt like the right thing to do, while he mopped up spilled beer that had pooled under a keg. He wasn't Nicole's boyfriend then.

When we finished cleaning up, he asked me if I wanted to smoke weed. We climbed the emergency stairwell on the outside of this old building on Mount Prospect and headed to the rooftop. Up there, he held my hand as we navigated small puddles of water and other debris. The rooftop was the kind of surface that made you feel aware of your body and its heaviness, aware of your center of gravity and its pull. With every step I felt as if the floor would cave in, but Evan gripped my hand even tighter, told me it was safe.

He lit a joint that we smoked while gazing at the stillness of Newark and the backdrop of New York City not far behind. The events that led to that kiss have blurred, but his hungry tongue wandering inside my mouth and the rush of his hands in and out of my shirt are as palpable now as they were then. Nothing came of that kiss. In fact, it was as if it had never happened.

And now he belongs to Nicole, who seems to be genetically predisposed to always get the biggest piece of pie.

Nicole looks in my direction. "We need to finish the project." Her cheeks are flushed pink.

I reach for my bag, which is now on the floor leaning against the wall. "We don't have to be in the same place at the same time to do that."

Nicole grabs her cardigan from the floor and drapes it over her shoulders. "Well, if you hadn't been in the bathroom for, like, thirty fucking minutes."

It's exactly during moments like these that I want to beat her up. But I know no one would forgive me. No one would understand. Also she would probably fight back. In the sixth grade she got suspended for punching this girl, Melanie, dead in the face. She told our family that Melanie was bullying her, but it was me who Melanie had been calling all sorts of names.

"I didn't know you needed me to hold your hand this whole time," I say.

She gets up from her seat and walks up to me, but Evan steps between us like a referee. His eyes plead with us to stop arguing.

Nicole's presence is suffocating, which is ironic, given the smallness of her body. It's not a single thing though. Sometimes it's the way she contorts her face into a variety of fake-nice expressions. Sometimes it's the waft of Dominican hair-salon smell—chemicals, heat, and burnt fibers—that's released when she does that performative hair flip. I can't seem to escape her. Not only are we related, but she's also my roommate.

I walk over to the opposite side of the room, where my laptop is charging. I yank the cord from the wall. I try to shove my laptop into my backpack, but it's so full that I can't make it fit. I take the laptop out, flip the backpack over, and watch as the contents spill onto the table in a really dramatic way that makes me look all angry and emotional.

"Y'all need to stop. We should've turned this in already," Evan says. He takes a deep breath, then bends over to pick up his backpack from the floor. His pants, too loose at the hips, are sagging. A mole the size of a raisin sits smack-dab in the middle of his lower back.

"I guess it doesn't matter at this point. I made plans, so I need to bounce," he says. He walks around the table and squeezes my shoulder before heading out of the room.

THE PROJECT IS a cue-to-cue itinerary of bonding activities and icebreakers for the incoming freshman class.

It isn't particularly hard. As with any group project, though, the problem is that you need to take others' input.

Back in our room, I open a spreadsheet and create several tabs. We're expected to camp at the Delaware Gap overnight. While the professors lead a few hours of instruction, we upperclassmen make sure the incoming freshmen are getting to know one another in more meaningful ways than just swapping spit.

I begin typing. I'm thinking of icebreakers, maybe Two Truths and a Lie to start. If the other Carmen were here, I imagine she'd be making decisions left and right without any regard for the inconsequential opinions of Evan and Nicole. *Fuck them*, she would probably say.

When I told Dr. Shrupka about the other Carmen, he said we all need role models. I nodded in agreement, though I was mostly distracted by his leather armchair—it could swallow him whole. He's tiny, with a thin, hollow face that looks even smaller behind thick-framed glasses. I could probably bench-press his ass, but that's beside the point. I told him what I love most about the other Carmen is her abandon. Where some women constrict their bodies into poses that bring absolutely no pleasure, the other Carmen doesn't. She fucks lazily; her languid body often melts into a tufted duvet, her limbs splayed unflatteringly. I mean, yes, I'm sure the sex is mostly staged. I'm sure the deliberate exchange of fluids isn't always real. I'm sure when the squeak of her voice subsides into heaving breaths, it's learned, like a dance routine committed to memory through arduous repetition. But even considering all of that, she exists comfortably. She looks happy.

I hear Nicole turn the key at the door, so I close my laptop. "What were you doing?" she asks in a singsongy voice that insinuates I've been caught. "Were you watching porn?" She removes her shoes at the door. Before I can get up, she jumps onto my bed and sits next to me. "I can tell you whatever you need to know."

I exhale and roll my eyes. "Please, teach me everything."

She gets up and sits on her bed. "You're such a bitch sometimes," she says. "That's why you can't get dick."

For as long as I can remember, Nicole and I have repelled each other like the same poles of two magnets. Rooming together is our latest attempt at building upon something that just doesn't exist. Like the rest of our family, Nicole pities me. The dark complexion of my skin, the layers of fat accumulating on my waist. But her insincere concern is more insulting than anything. I'd much rather lick an armpit or stub a toe than listen to her give me advice on men.

"Maybe I don't want any," I say.

"You gay?"

"Sure, Nicole. You done?"

She walks over to her closet and pulls out a small duffel bag. "I'm spending the night at Evan's."

THE OTHER CARMEN is wearing clear stripper heels, a modern-day rendition of glass slippers. They're tall, five or six inches by the looks of them. They seem impossible to walk in, which seems irrelevant because she's on her knees again, crawling on the floor and purring like a cat. I switch tabs and share the itinerary with the adviser. I don't cc Nicole or Evan because they didn't do the work. I go back to the other Carmen. The shot has switched to a closeup of her face, capturing details I hadn't quite noticed before: a narrow gap between her front teeth, sandpaper acne underneath caked-on makeup. Her dark skin shines beneath a layer of body oil. She continues to crawl until she reaches a pole. While still on her knees, she arches her back and spreads her legs; a heart-shaped gem, blue like the pendant from *Titanic*, peeks out from inside her rectum.

The camera zooms in to reveal stretch marks spreading like tree branches from her ass to her thighs. Still, the other Carmen remains as confident as if there were no imperfections exposed. She grips the pole tighter and pulls herself up. Standing tall on her glass slippers, she smiles. I close the browser and head for the closet, where I pick out a pair of leggings and a crop top I bought on a whim months ago. The crop top leaves *all* of my midriff exposed. For a second I don't recognize my own naked flesh, bulging like the filling of an overstuffed cookie sandwich or a hamburger patty much too big for the bun. I take a deep breath. I just want, for a brief moment in time, not to give a fuck.

The walk to the Equal Opportunity Fund's office is mostly pleasant, except for the sanitation workers that whistle at me the moment I turn the corner. The Rutgers campus sits in the middle of Downtown Newark. It is a microcosm within the city, close enough to a couple of parks, a few restaurants, a new Whole Foods, a new Starbucks, and some fancy residentials where gentrifiers live. On a summer day like this one, it's mostly empty, except for high school Upward Bound students. Outside the quad a group of international kids unload their luggage from a charter bus; they're part of a summer program that will take them to every tourist trap in New York City while cutting costs by having them stay here in Newark.

At the EOF's office, Whitney, a senior and a program adviser, is hunched over the front desk and thumbing through her phone. "Hey, girl. Look at you!"

"Look at me!" I flash a grin, aware that neither my face nor the tone of my voice conveys genuine enthusiasm.

"Cute top," she says. "I've never seen you wear a crop top before."

"Thanks."

At her desk there's one of those single-serve blender cups filled with a thick green concoction. She takes a sip, then licks some of the residue from her top lip.

"What's that?" I ask just to make conversation.

"Oh, you know, a smoothie cleanse. Trying to shed a few pounds, as usual." She takes another sip. "You want the recipe?"

I don't want the damn recipe. Truth is, I've done every diet out there. Once in the tenth grade I survived solely off cabbage soup for two weeks in preparation for Nicole's quinceañera. Every time I opened the soup container, it was as if I'd released a fart bomb. My mom and brother would clear the area, cackling on their way out. No one gave much thought to the fact that I had to eat said fart bomb. At the end of my two-week starvation diet, I managed to squeeze into the too-small dress only to have the zipper snap open the night of the party. Cabbage soup was followed by Master Cleanse, which was followed by Atkins, and so on. I gave up on that. Besides, Dr. Shrupka says it's more important that I focus on the things that make me happy. Whatever those are.

I smile and ask her for the keys to the supply closet.

"Evan is in there," she says.

The supply closet is big; I imagine it can fit about a dozen people. Though there isn't any ventilation in there, it's surprisingly cool. I find Evan sitting on the floor and leaning against a bookshelf, sulking. I walk over and gently kick his foot. He doesn't even look up.

"What's wrong with you?"

He extends his arm toward me as if expecting me to help him up, which I do.

"I broke up with your cousin," he says.

I grab an empty box from a shelf and begin dumping in everything that may come in handy on the overnight trip: index cards, pens, toilet paper, a couple of inflatable balls still in their original packaging. Their breakup doesn't surprise me. I don't even know what else they do besides hook up. I mean, that's fun and all, but then what happens?

"You hear me?" he says.

"I heard you. I'm sorry."

"It's okay." He hands over a ball of rubber bands. "These could be useful, right?"

I dump it into the box. He has yet to ask whether I turned in the project, though I'm sure he knows I did.

"Have you talked to Nicole?" he asks.

"No." It's uncomfortable thinking about Nicole moping around. Not the idea of Nicole moping around per se, but more the question of whether I'm supposed to care, or whether I'm supposed to feel bad for her, which I decidedly don't. If anything, it's quite the opposite, and I'm not sure what kind of person that makes me. A shitty cousin? A jealous friend?

Evan's eyes linger on me. I tug the hem of my top down, but it's not long enough to cover my belly.

"She's probably looking for you," he says. I look at my phone: nothing. "She probably needs someone to talk to."

"Yeah, I don't know why that would be me."

I STOP BY the room to pack for the trip to the Delaware Gap. Nicole's on her bed, painting her toenails bubble-gum pink. The room smells like a Yankee Candle store mixed with Penn Station popcorn.

Her long hair is tied into a high bun, and a few strands frame her face. Even when she's presumably heartbroken, she's unnervingly beautiful. "Hey," she says, placing the bottle of polish on her night table.

"You okay?" I ask. Nicole and I have never confided in each other or sought each other's comfort; she never seems to need it.

In our family, if you are Nicole, you're told how impressive it is that you're accomplishing so much:

juggling an academic life with extracurriculars, keeping your body in perfect shape and your hair long and straight—even if that's only made possible by formaldehyde and a flat iron set at four hundred degrees. If you are me, you're diagnosed with fealdad: ugliness that manifests itself in darker skin, extra weight, and curly hair. You're prescribed a diet and steady sessions of deep-conditioning treatments at the Dominican hair salon.

"Not really," she says. "Evan broke up with me."

"He told me this morning." On TV, Lizzo responds to vitriol about her twerking. She flips a long ponytail over her shoulder. Nicole watches her. Her mouth gapes in awe.

"She gives no fucks," she says, looking up at me.

"Why should she?"

"You know why." She grabs a cotton swab and dips it into a bottle of nail-polish remover. She wipes the skin surrounding her toenails, then leans back to examine her feet. "I didn't know you and Evan were close like that," she adds. And there it is, that uptick in her voice, a warning for me to stay away. "What else did he tell you?"

"Nothing else," I say. "We're not friends like that."

Nicole doesn't know Evan and I kissed that night. I've thought about telling her. But my guess is she'll think I'm making it up.

THE DELAWARE WATER GAP is an hour and thirty minutes from Newark. Folks in charge assume we don't go out to the woods much, so there's always an outdoors trip with the intent of exposing us Black and brown students to life outside the "hood." Every year I go, I'm reminded that I love nature almost as much as I hate people.

We meet on the lawn outside the dorms. The incoming class is small, which is fortuitous because it means there is less work for us to do. Fewer heads to keep track of. Though we are only a few years older than them, the age gap feels incredibly wide, as if we, at twenty, are full-fledged adults caring for very small children.

Evan comes out to join the rest of us. He's wearing a pair of gray sweatpants and a white T-shirt, green backpack slung over his shoulder. He smiles. I wave at him and smile back.

He skips over a puddle of mud on the lawn and leans forward for a hug.

"How are you doing?" I ask.

"I feel great."

I look behind us, wondering if Nicole is coming anytime soon. The bus leaves in thirty minutes.

"Where's your cousin?" he asks.

It's possible she decided not to come at all. I can't blame her. If it were me in her place and the man I was probably in love with but no longer dating was expected to be with me in a remote location overnight, I wouldn't go either.

"I'm not sure she's coming," I say.

The students eagerly board the bus and head straight to the back. Evan jumps in and asks everyone to move to the front. Advisers will be sitting in the back. He steps off the bus. "We don't need that kind of stress," he says.

Realistically we can't police them the whole time or stop them from hooking up. It's what you do on this sort of trip—you hook up.

He grabs my backpack off the sidewalk and asks me where to put it. I shrug as we board the bus, hoping he places it wherever he'll be sitting, and he does just that.

"Do you want the window or the aisle?" he asks.

I feel heat spreading through my forehead. I'm not a small girl. The expanse of my hips makes it so I can't just plop in anywhere, especially if I'm sitting close to someone.

I say "whatever," and he points to the window. I take the seat knowing I'll be trapped and at the mercy of just how close he wants to be.

We leave without Nicole. Once on the road, Evan takes his phone from his pocket. Earbuds go in, and I'm relieved he won't have to listen to my anxiety-induced shortness of breath. Only after resting my face against the window do I notice that it's stained with fingerprints. I'm unable to move because Evan is slumped, leaning on me, his head resting in the nook between my face and neck, his Winterfresh breath blowing gently. My stomach is fluttering. Why is he so close to me? Should I rest my head on his? Should I place my hand on his knee? I think the other Carmen would. She would take charge and assert her presence.

THE SCHOOL BOOKED a few cabins at a recreational site. Mrs. Williams, the program supervisor, hands Evan and me a folder with room assignments. She and the rest of the coordinators share a cabin across from ours. Evan and I have to sleep in the same cabin as the freshmen. We huddle outside in a circle, and Mrs. Williams goes over the rules and expectations. She tells us we are free to explore as long as we are all back by 8 p.m. sharp for the bonfire and s'mores.

The cabin is dark inside and smells faintly of damp wood. Twin bunk beds and a couple of dressers fill every room. There's no decor on the walls except for a clock that seems more practical than ornamental. An old white wood-burning stove sits in the corner of the common room next to a window. The inside of the stove is pristine, almost like it's never been used. In the closet near the kitchenette, there are two small space heaters. I try to imagine what it would be like to come here on a romantic getaway during the winter, when the trail is covered in ice and snow and your body seeks warmth the most.

Evan and I are in separate rooms, across from each other. He suggests we go on a hike, then steps inside his room, drops his backpack on the bed, and takes off his pants. The door is still open. I stare, and he sees me staring before stretching his arm and pushing the door closed.

The more I think of Evan, the wetter I get. For a moment I consider lying on the bed and masturbating. Maybe what I need is some post-orgasm clarity to take the edge off. Then I'll be able to go for a hike like a normal human being. But I don't have time for all that. I wipe myself down, put on a fresh pair of underwear, and put the leggings back on. I grab a plastic nip of Jack Daniel's I've been keeping at the bottom of my backpack. I tilt my head back, taking in as much as I can handle at once. Goosebumps flare up and down my arms, but I keep gulping until I finish it. I reach inside my shirt to readjust my breasts so that they spill over my sports bra just a little. I let my hair loose and move it to the side. The full-body mirror hanging off the door is covered in a thin film of dust, so I get closer and take a good look at myself. This body and this face are all I have. It's not an affirmation. It's a fact.

When I open the door, Evan is standing right there, holding a travel mug. He shakes it gingerly, and I laugh.

"This cute girl I know keeps her weed inside her coffee mug."

"Corny," I say.

"I was talking about you." He takes a step closer, his teeth flashing.

"I know."

"So what's corny about it?" He takes another step.

"You, trying to flirt with me."

He unscrews the top and holds it under my nose. "I bet you can't wait."

ON THE TRAIL, we walk past a middle-aged white couple jogging with an overweight lab lagging behind them. We leave the trail and head toward the woods. The farther away from the river, the quieter it gets. We keep walking, looking behind us every now and then just in case there are students nearby.

On my left ankle a red welt forms, and I stop to scratch it. Evan turns around. "It's just a bite," I tell him.

"Put your leg up on my knee," he says. I shift my weight to my right leg and steady myself by holding on to a branch. The tight grip of his hand on my calf makes my heartbeat quicken. With his fingernail, he digs into my skin and forms a cross over the bite. "It'll stop itching soon." I put my leg down and watch him dust off his pants.

We sit next to each other on the ground with our backs against a tree. He takes out a joint from the coffee mug and lights it. I take a drag and exhale, then pass it back to him. He puffs, then begins coughing violently.

"Rookie," I say.

The vastness of the woods swallows the words between us. I turn my head, following the sounds of leaves rustling and small animals scurrying about. Everything becomes louder. Evan inches closer and holds my face. He kisses me. His lips linger on mine, and I feel my shoulders drop. He touches my thighs and yanks me forward. I move my hand inside his shirt to caress his back, but he moves it and places it on his erection. I want him to slow down.

"Have you ever fucked in the woods?"

His question gives me pause, jolts me out of the moment. It felt as if we had been swaying to the rhythm of this song, then the music stopped abruptly. I can't get past the logistics. Am I supposed to remove my pants and let the bugs crawl over my naked skin? Or get on all fours, my bare knees pressed against rocks as if I were kneeling on rice? I think of the other Carmen, and as hard as I try, I can't recall her fucking in the woods. I can't picture her on the dirt, twigs digging into her skin. A warm, wet hole and not a person.

"Have you?" he asks again before leaning in for another kiss. While kissing me, he pulls out his wallet and takes out a condom. He shoves the little golden square inside his front pocket. I pretend not to notice the sleight of hand. He presses against me, breathless, like we're running out of time. But I don't feel the same rush. His body suddenly feels like dead weight.

I've never made love. No one's ever made love to me. Not the way I imagine it, anyway. Sex always happens like this: with me half-dressed and in a haze, on twin beds, under stairwells, in closets, on bunk beds, under blankets, in public bathrooms, and, yes, in the woods. Sex has always been circumstantial. It's been noise. But you can't fill a void with sound alone. A loud empty room is still empty.

Evan's hand slowly approaches my face. One second it's floating in the air, the next it's touching my cheek.

"Hey, are you okay?" he asks.

My head is spinning.

When I open my eyes, I see Evan staring at me. His hand is now on my forehead, as if taking my temperature. He leans in closer and kisses me again. I realize that my helplessness is alluring. His mouth trails from my bottom lip to the side of my neck. He nibbles on my earlobe. I stare past him and watch a couple of birds fluttering, one behind the other. His lips work their way back up to my mouth.

I hold my hand up to his face, and he immediately retreats. "I'm sorry," he says. "I thought you wanted this."

I thought I did too. He looks the other way and bites the inside of his cheek. He gets up from the ground and offers me a hand, which he takes back before I can even stretch my arm out. I hold on to a stubby root protruding from the dirt and use it to pull myself up.

"Can you walk on your own?" he asks.

"I need a moment." I take a deep breath and remind myself that soon enough I will be sober and this will be over. In a few days I will be sitting in Dr. Shrupka's office. I will tell him about the trip, about Evan in the woods, about the weed and the Jack Daniels, and about Nicole.

Evan grabs the coffee mug, puts it back inside his backpack, and begins to walk.

I hold on to the trunk of every tree and follow the sound of his footsteps. He looks back and tells me to grab onto his arm if I need to. I don't. He says he won't touch me unless I ask. He is distant and impersonal, as if I've done something wrong. The closer we get to the cabin, the longer his strides become. But I don't feel the need to catch up. I know where I'm going.

Love Language

MY MOTHER ALWAYS SAYS THAT A DROP OF WATER, IF persistent enough, will hollow out a stone. That a squeaky wheel, if loud enough, will get greased. As I watch Rodrigo struggle to chew a forkful of spaghetti too big for his mouth, I wonder if I'm the wheel that squeaks or the water that drops.

Rodrigo's doing that thing where he tries to force a smile out of politeness. I'm sure he hates the food, but it's likely he won't tell me. I watch him stab at a neat little pile drenched in the garlic-infused olive oil I got at the bodega. He holds the spoon with his left hand, the fork with his right. He twirls the fork around hastily, gathering so many noodles you'd think we had a damn thing to do after dinner.

"What's wrong?" I ask, though I'm aware of just how much is wrong. For one, the clams are from a can that sat on a dusty shelf. Yes, there's a seafood market down the street, where sacks of fresh clams crowd a U-shaped countertop, but if I were to buy fresh clams and dinner were to be delicious, or even edible, Rodrigo would still just sit there, ignoring me.

We weren't always like this. The honeymoon period ended, and I guess other things died along the way. It's hard to say what exactly. Change is imperceptible sometimes. That is, until it grows and accumulates. Before you know it, a nuisance becomes a problem, and a leak becomes a flood. You could say Rodrigo and I are standing in a puddle of water. Our socks are getting wet. And I'm wondering if we still have a chance.

Rodrigo looks at me. A noodle dangles from the corner of his mouth. He slurps it up. "Nothing's wrong," he says.

Months ago, I sought my mother's advice. I asked her if she and my father still spoke each other's love languages. She cackled so loudly I had to move the phone away from my face. She said, "That's some white people shit."

I take a sip of wine and stare at his eyes. His crow's feet make his eyes look smaller than they are. Maybe it's not that they're so small but that his forehead protrudes and his eyes are sunken, making him look more somber than he is.

"You hate it," I say.

"I don't."

"Yes, you do."

"Fine."

The hard cast holding the broken pieces of my tibia together is making my skin itch. I use a butter knife to scratch my leg. Rodrigo watches me but doesn't say a word.

"So what's wrong with the food?"

I wait for him to swallow the thick bulge of spaghetti he's been chewing. Why can't he see that I crave the sound of his voice? I'm expecting a straight answer, one that will let me know what he hates most: the garlic, the gummy chunks passing as clams, or me. He finally swallows. "I think it would have been better if you'd used fresh garlic or fresh herbs," he says.

He's right. The dish is oily. The garlic tastes artificial. And who can forget about the clams? He puts his fork down and pushes the plate toward the middle of the table. It makes a faint scraping noise as it slides across the polished wood.

"You're not going to finish it?"

He looks at me, drags the plate back, retrieves his fork, and then stabs at the little mound. Shoving noodles into his mouth, he chews them awkwardly, his mouth partially open. "Did you know Gabe and Carla have been growing tomatoes and herbs in the courtyard?" he says. "They share with everyone."

"I'm well aware."

"Then why don't you go out there and grab some herbs, or help or something?"

I don't mean to sneer, but I do. "I have a broken leg. Remember?"

"You seem to pick and choose when that's a problem."

He could be referring to the fact that we haven't had sex since I broke my leg. Or the fact that I spend a couple of hours every day at the Portuguese bar down the street from our apartment. It's a short walk and about the only movement I get since I've been stuck here. My spending time at the bar bothers Rodrigo, though he has yet to explicitly tell me so.

Though I've tried, I can't remember a time when our conversations didn't sound like this. Our relationship has corroded like a cheap necklace exposed to the elements. We barely speak. I don't want to fuck someone who barely speaks to me.

I get up from the table. My crutches are leaning against the wall next to me, but I don't grab them. I hop the short distance to the trash bin and dump the leftover spaghetti. I hop back to the table and grab Rodrigo's plate, then dump his spaghetti too. The clatter of the plates in the sink and the thumping of every hop exasperate him. I can hear his heavy exhale.

"You want your crutches?" he asks.

"What for?"

He grabs the crutches and brings them over to me, placing them against the side of the couch. "My jacket smells like garlic," he says.

"That's a shame."

He knows I don't mean it. I could have turned the fan on or opened the windows to let out the densely fragrant air. It's thick and pungent and hard to breathe. But with every petty argument, I dig; I search for Rodrigo, for a spark in his stoic face, in his absentminded touch. I find glimmers of emotion in his sarcastic tones, in the way he rolls his eyes or scoffs. I find a man there. So I keep coming back to him.

That day on the phone, after she laughed at me, my mother mentioned rituals. Did I try wearing a red thong for twenty-four hours, then boiling said thong along with a pair of my beloved's underwear? Did I place a figurine of San Antonio—upside down, because otherwise it won't work—on top of a bed of flowers? And did I say a prayer asking for my beloved's eternal devotion? From her tone, I gathered she thought I hadn't done enough.

Rodrigo grabs the jacket, then turns the corner to our bedroom. I turn on the television and mindlessly flip through channels. It's what I do most these days. I sit there and put my leg up on the coffee table and give in to the monotony of TV. A short while back, before I broke my leg on a trampoline trying to do something exciting with Rodrigo, I'd mocked people like my downstairs neighbor, Gabe, for watching so much drama.

Gabe also spends a lot of time at home. He's a writer and, from what I can hear through the vents, a fan of soap operas and game shows. He and his wife, also in their thirties, have tried to befriend us, but I'm not fond of Carla. There's this bohemian thing about her that makes me want to pull her hair. When she talks, she smiles too much and nods repeatedly and paraphrases your sentences to let you know what a good listener she is.

On TV, a group of contestants on *MasterChef* gear up for a three-layer-cake baking challenge. They sprint to the pantry. The oldest contestant brims with excitement. Basket in hand, she picks out an array of ingredients: berries, mint, heavy whipping cream. She's a self-taught baker who has been selling cakes to the parishioners at her local church for a decade. Cake is her love language. She mixes the batter by hand, leaning into it with the full weight of her shoulders. After the cakes rest, she pipes on the cream, smooths it out, then stacks one layer at a time. She arranges an assortment of berries and finishes with a light dusting of confectioners' sugar. The judges bite in, undoing in mere seconds what took so long to put together.

The futility of all that effort.

Behind the chatter of the TV, I hear the forceful clacking of Rodrigo's fingers against the keyboard. The *tap tap tap* of the backspace key makes it from our bedroom to the living room. There's no point in asking what he's writing. Emails? Memos? Invoices for the hotel? He will be pounding away until the green glow of the clock on the cable box shows eleven. A minute or so after, he will come out of our room for some whiskey, which he will drink in a single gulp before heading off to sleep.

The weight of my head pulls me forward. My eyes open and close, and open and close. I've been sleeping on the couch for three months. Our bed was already too high for me, and now it's almost impossible to climb onto it with the hard cast on my leg.

You could say there were signs all along. Endless bickering followed by long periods of silence. Fissures we spackled and painted over. When you're love-buzzed and twenty, you think you can make it through anything. But then ten years go by and you find yourself at a trampoline park, a lousy date you planned trying to recapture the glee you felt years ago, and on that trampoline you close your eyes because it feels like you're flying—until you land awkwardly, hearing nothing but the snap of a bone.

I turn off the TV. I get under the blanket and squint at the lamp next to the couch. I watch the ring of colors that forms in the light until it begins to blur. I wonder if Rodrigo is thinking of me.

AFTER RODRIGO LEAVES for work in the morning, I decide to get basil from the courtyard. Tonight I'll make something fresh, something he might love, like a watermelon basil salad, to start. Maybe if I make an effort, this evening will be different. It's what my mother would do. It's what she did when my father left us.

When I was a kid, my father moved out of the house for some time. He'd fallen in love with a woman at work. Her name was Rosalina. She spoke in a soft voice and always made eye contact. We would run into her at church, and at the laundromat, and at the bakery. She would make my father an elaborate upside-down pineapple flan every year for his birthday. And so every year we savored that flan, plucking the maraschino cherries one by one, dipping our fingers in the caramel that pooled at the bottom of the pan.

My father's decision to leave nearly broke my mother, but she was determined to get him back. One day she walked into our kitchen holding a piece of paper with "Rosalina" written on it. She grabbed a lighter, then set the paper on fire. I watched the flame eat every cursive loop. Later that week she wrote my father's name on the bottoms of her shoes and wore them for hours, pacing back and forth, each step an imploration.

I get dressed and head toward the back door of our apartment. I rarely use the back door. Rodrigo uses it when he tries to sneak out for a smoke, but he forgets this is an old building and everything creaks. I descend the back stairwell, careful not to fall on my face. It's a spiral staircase that starts out wide and then narrows like a cornucopia. I can fit with my crutches, but it isn't comfortable, and I wonder whether it'd be faster and safer if I hold on to both rails and hop carefully.

I set the crutches down, and they slip through a gap between steps. They hit the floor and bounce just a little. The noise echoes, which brings Gabe running out of his apartment. I mumble under my breath. I don't feel like talking to Gabe, or anyone. My good leg is unshaven, and I'm not wearing a bra. My boobs sag a bit, and my eyebrows need brushing. My mother would say I've given up.

Back then my mother was relentless. When the steps she'd taken didn't yield results, she shaved her curls and began wearing a white scarf wrapped tightly around her head. She'd wear a white skirt cinched at the waist and a white blouse with sleeves that would open up like wings as she waltzed through our living room, chanting in a language that was neither English nor Spanish. She was a living Santeria doll.

I look down, and Gabe is already at the foot of the stairs. "I'm okay!" I say, but he's skipped two steps and is running up to me.

"Let me help you," he says. "How do you want to do this?" Gabe has a beautiful smile. It's white and bright and surrounded by dimples that make him look younger than he is.

"I can carry you down," he insists.

"You don't have to do that."

"Please."

He has a tattoo of an anchor on his right bicep. It's a bit faded and the lines are uneven. And he has veiny, manly hands. They're so different from Rodrigo's.

He squeezes in so that we're side by side. I grab his waist and he holds mine. His shirt is damp, and I can feel heat emanating through the cotton fabric. It doesn't bother me, but he addresses it anyway. "I'm sweaty as hell." I giggle to make him feel comfortable, or to make myself feel comfortable—I don't know.

"No worries. Have you looked at me?"

Gabe says, "I wasn't going to say anything, but since you brought it up."

He winks at me and I'm reminded of the men at the bar. They wink too, and ask about my day, and try to pay for my drinks, and accidentally brush up against my leg. For the few hours I'm there, I'm interesting. Everyone wants to talk to me.

I look at Gabe. "My good leg is stubbly."

He pauses and gives me a funny look. "I don't mind hair."

I weigh the words coming out of his mouth and realize I don't know him well enough to know if this is who he normally is. And I don't trust myself enough to tell whether this is or isn't a mirage.

He brings me to the foot of the stairs and grabs my crutches, then opens the screen door that leads to the courtyard. He extends his hand and I take it, even though I'm okay to hold on to the wall. I notice he hasn't asked about Rodrigo, and I won't ask about his wife. I imagine she's at work, but I'm not sure I care. Gabe's built several raised beds in the garden. Lumber scraps nailed to one another and painted picket-fence white. Tomatoes, peppers, cucumbers, scallions, and basil grow in the direction of the sun. Near the metal fence that separates our yard from the neighbor's, he keeps potted perennials.

"Help me water these guys," he says, pointing at the asters springing from a raised bed made from a repurposed car tire. I tell him I'm impressed. He tells me anybody can do this, but that isn't true. Not everyone can keep things alive.

I hop forward and seek out his hand. He hands me the hose and I struggle to find my balance, so he holds me by the waist once again. I feel the grip of each finger. Then I feel my body pulsing just about everywhere. Before I know it, I imagine his hands prying my legs open.

I grab the hose firmly, but as Gabe cranks up the water, I lose control and end up watering myself instead. Water trickles down my torso and I catch myself laughing like a child on a school playground. I can't stop looking at his face. I grab the hose and point it at him. The stream of water hits him, and he gasps. "Oh, yeah?" he says. He pulls it from me and hoses me down. He bends forward, holding his chest as he laughs. The cold water feels like a jolt, so I lose myself in the unbridled joy of the moment. Then I realize my cast is soaked.

"Shit," he says. The spigot on the wall is rusty, and it squeaks when he shuts off the water. He rolls up the hose and hangs it on a hook. I look up to the building to see if any neighbors have seen us. Looks like it's just the two of us.

"Let me get you a towel." He looks concerned. His frowning tells me he feels guilty about the water in my cast, which is now squishing inside, making me want to split the cast in two.

I sit on the bench, wet. Gabe makes it back holding a towel and a robe. Before I ask, he says the robe is his and not his wife's. When he drapes the robe over my shoulders, his hands linger. I stare and welcome the transgression with a smile, a wordless invitation. He steps closer. For a brief second it feels as if we're sharing the same breath. I don't say anything when he smooths out the lapel and his hand brushes against my breast. I don't say anything until my heart beats faster, and it feels as if the sun has moved closer.

"I better go." I grip the handles of my crutches firmly. Remembering the herbs, I bend over to yank a handful of basil. I hold it between my teeth, then head to the door.

Gabe looks at me. "See you soon?" he asks.

I nod.

I think of my mother and wonder if she thinks it was all worth it. My father did eventually come back—after she drove us to the live poultry market, where we bought the fattest chicken. At home she wrung its neck, cut off its head, and drained the blood. She cooked and ate it, slurping its juice and licking its grease, her tongue tracing a path from knuckle to nail.

I'll Give You a Reason

I MET MARIA BACK IN THE FIFTH GRADE. SHE WAS THIS skinny girl whose mom would always pack her salami sandwiches for lunch. When I think of Maria today, I think of those slices of salami stuffed inside a hardened kaiser roll. No lettuce, tomatoes, or cheese. Just belch-inducing salami.

This was back when Mom was buying me outfits two sizes too small. That year I was hungry all the time. It must have been why I couldn't help but notice Maria's sharp bones poking through the white short-sleeved uniform shirt, and the thick black leather belt that secured her pants by cinching her tiny waist. She seemed small in more ways than one.

No one picked on Maria. Still, that didn't stop her from crying every single day. The most insignificant things—things that didn't matter to any of us—would make her cry, as if her spirit was as thin and as frail as her body.

At first she would try to keep her crying to herself by putting her slick face down on the desk. Me and the kids sitting near her would push our desks closer to hers and ask, "Maria, what's wrong?" or "Why are you crying?"

141

And she'd say something like she couldn't find her pencil sharpener. And I would think, it's just a sharpener, but I never said that out loud. Instead I'd ask, "What does it look like?" and would then set out to meander around the classroom, pretending to look for it.

But it wasn't always about the sharpener. Some reason unknown to all of us would send Maria to that place inside her head where tears were abundant and free-flowing. Everyone would gather around her like the Santa Maria Madre de Dios that she wasn't.

If Maria hadn't cried by lunchtime, I would anxiously wait for her to begin. Her tears lit me up like a flare gun in the dark. When Maria went a week without crying, the world felt off-kilter. I once took that same sharpener from her desk, wrapped it in loose-leaf paper, then tossed it in the trash. I watched as she cried for her missing sharpener. I began to wonder what would happen if I took something bigger—a notebook, her pencil case, a salami sandwich. How much would she cry then? That was the year I bled through my gym shorts while running laps around the basketball court. Everyone laughed. Mr. Sandford sent me to the nurse to take care of my "business." After that day, I wasn't required to play or participate in any activity I didn't want to. Maybe because she cried all the time and Mr. Sandford didn't want to deal with any drama, Maria, too, was allowed to sit out on the bleachers. Most days we sat in silence and watched the rest of the class play broom hockey or volleyball. We rarely talked. At times I'd catch her staring at me as if looking for something.

At home I wanted to tell everyone about Maria and how she cried every day for either no reason whatsoever or for things that shouldn't matter. But my parents were in the middle of a screaming match, and my sister wasn't home. So I sat on my bed and wondered where her tears came from, how they streamed down her little face with no end in sight. I wanted to know what it felt like to tap into that well so easily. Did she feel lighter?

I thought of all the sad things I knew, like my grandma passing away on her bed in the DR, her yellowed skin, her thinning hair pulled into a low ponytail. Then I thought of my best friend Luna and her family moving back to Brazil because they didn't have papers. They left without even saying goodbye.

I pushed next on my CD player until Alanis Morrisette's "Uninvited" came on. And just for a brief moment I felt *it*, building up in my chest, working its way up to my throat. Before I could hold on to it long enough to release it, I heard my mother's voice in my head: *What do you have to cry for? I'll give you a reason.* I imagined her standing in front of me. Beautiful, svelte, and strong.

ONE DAY DURING PE, Maria asked if I wanted to come over. Whether my parents gave me permission or not, I knew I had to go. I needed to know what swelled and pushed against her throat.

She lived above the local pet shop, in the heart of the Ironbound along a busy commercial strip near seafood restaurants and Portuguese bakeries. The place had a blue awning and a wood-pallet sign adorned with hand-painted puppies, kittens, snakes, and cockatoos like illustrations from a coloring book. For years I'd walked by the store, stopping at the glass window to look at whichever animal they'd put on display that week, not knowing that people lived above. Inside there was a long narrow hallway with kennels stacked against each wall. It was brightly lit and smelled like a bag of kibbles.

"Come this way," Maria said. She was wearing baggy denim overalls. It occurred to me that I'd never seen her without our school uniform. In those plain clothes, she looked as regular as anyone else.

At the register, a lady eyed me up and down before waving hello. Her grin appeared and disappeared from her face before I could even say hi. She leaned on the counter and looked in our direction. "¿Qué vas a hacer con ella?"

Maria kept walking. "I'm just going to show her around," she responded before grabbing my hand. "Do you want to help me feed the snakes?"

I nodded and followed. Besides that movie, *Anaconda*, the only other snake I could think of was a garden snake that I'd watched my grandma sweep away with a broom. That was in her house in La Romana a year ago, before she became so sick she couldn't sweep anymore.

Maria turned back around as if to see if I was still following her. She stared me down. "Why do you take my stuff?" Under the hallway's fluorescent lights her eyes were a deep brown, so dark they seemed almost black. "I know it's you."

Her question made me pause. I didn't think she had noticed. It was just that one time.

She picked up a stick and used it to prop up the lid of the tank. The snake uncoiled its body and slithered against the pane, slowly moving its head up toward us. I watched in silence as Maria ran her fingers along its skin. "Do you want to touch it?" she asked. "It feels like a purse or a shoe."

I shook my head. I didn't have the courage to touch it. She held up the snake with both arms and took a step toward me. Her arms were suspended in the air as if waiting for a partner to join her in a dance. She clasped her index fingers together and then twirled slowly like a ballerina. The snake hung from her arms. Only its head curved upward like a tiny *s*.

She placed it back inside the tank. "Hang on," she said, then walked past a curtain that sectioned off the room. I stood there in the same spot where I'd been standing the whole time and watched the snake curl itself back into a coil.

When Maria came back, she was holding something in her hands. "You're gonna wanna see this," she said. She brought her hands up to my chest and opened them just enough so that I could see the blurry movement of something white squirming inside.

"I don't want to see this."

She looked at me and held the mouse by its tail. "You have to," she said, then dropped the mouse into the tank. It only took a few seconds for the snake to unravel like a whip. It clamped the mouse mid-run, then wrapped itself around its body. It tightened its grip until the mouse's feet stopped kicking and its tail hung limp off to the side. I heard the faintest squeak before Maria moved the stick out of the way and closed the lid.

"Don't touch my shit," she said.

There I felt *it* again, swelling up in my throat. It poured out of me like water from a broken fire hydrant. I ran out of the store and all the way down the street to my house.

I stopped at the corner to take a deep breath. I inhaled and exhaled. I counted to ten. My mom's car was parked outside the house, so I drew my arm up to my face and wiped it dry with the back of my sleeve.

Something Larger, Something Whole

THE WIFE PREPARED FOR THEIR VISIT BY DEEP CLEANING the rug, a wedding present symbolizing fortune and happiness. Wrapped and sealed in a black tarp, the rug had arrived at the home of the young couple, where it was greeted with a side-eye and a subtle wrinkle of the mouth. At eight-by-ten feet, it covered the entire living room floor, from the nicked mahogany desk that served as their TV stand to the ripped-up leather couch where they ate dinner in silence most nights. It was extravagant, and it looked out of place in the small one-bedroom apartment. The price tag had been left on—as either an explicit reminder admonishing the couple against mistreating the gift or a faux pas highlighting the sacrifices made to ensure its existence. Either way, for the price of the rug, they thought, they could have gone on a honeymoon—a tradition better suited for their kind of love.

A year's worth of labor had been devoted to hand-knotting the rug's wool and silk fabrics. It was custom-made by a villager whose blessings had bestowed two generations before them the gift of a harmonious union strong enough to withstand the blow of desire.

The mother of the wife had explained the arduous weaving process in detail, from the moment the villager chose the fibers to the long hours she spent spinning the materials. Every thread in the fabric, the mother told them, surrendered itself in order to become something larger, something whole. But the young couple couldn't see for themselves the value of the piece. It was beyond them. The rug's intricate patterns told a story in a language neither the wife nor the husband could yet speak.

The rug was never beautiful, the wife complained. Its flowers and leaves and crowded paisley patterns were at times incomprehensible, other times meaningless. The parents' lectures and talks about their own rugs couldn't help the couple find beauty in the lifeless object that required a level of attention and care they didn't know how to give.

Now, two short years after its arrival, it had become uglier. Its striking hues of red and maroon were fading before the young couple's eyes; with each passing day the intensity of the colors became duller. Sunlight blazed through their window, turning the dark greens into shades of brown and yellow. Now the rug just sat there, deteriorated and overwhelmed with neglect: neglect that had turned into abuse.

The hapless rug suffered wounds: wounds inflicted with intent; wounds perpetrated by carelessness; wounds as casual as spilled milk; wounds by the husband; wounds by the wife; wounds masquerading as accidents; wounds pleading for forgiveness; wounds saying, "It won't happen again."

The first stain could be traced back to a screaming match that awakened the neighbors, and to the glass of red wine that sat too close to the edge of the table and tumbled and spilled over the light-brown clusters of paisleys. The wife attempted to clean it by mixing baking soda and dish detergent. This being the first wound, she tried with genuine effort to heal it. But the baking soda and the dish detergent, compounded by the vigorous effort of regret, left a discolored patch that, much to the couple's dismay, just wouldn't disappear.

There was also that funky smell permeating the bottom right quadrant. It came after the dog ate and then vomited an entire pizza that was unattended on the coffee table. That, too, left a stain.

A third stain made its appearance shortly after. It consisted of drops of the wife's favorite nail polish. Neither she nor the husband could remember who'd thrown the polish at the wall, when the bottle had shattered, or where it had sprinkled the bright purple liquid. Occasionally she'd find and pick at the dried-up droplets of paint, hoping, rather passively, that one day they would come off.

Today, with the impending questions and looming disappointment of their parents, they decided to address the problem. They rented a steam cleaner and bought industrial-grade soap, determined to get rid of the stains, no matter how futile the effort. While waiting for the store clerk to retrieve the machine, the couple held hands and exchanged kisses in an aisle at Home Depot. Their smiles, nervous and ephemeral, hid the fact that there were only a few hours left to repair the damage. They both questioned how they ended up there, waiting, avoiding each other's gazes, and dodging the thought that maybe it was time to let go of the rug.

Boxes

YOU WAKE UP AND MAKE OATMEAL. YOU SLICE A COUPLE of bananas—too ripe for your liking, but Noah loves them that way, when their skins are dotted with brown spots.

You sprinkle a bit of salt, add sugar and a teaspoon of cinnamon. It's only 9 a.m. Noah won't be here for at least twenty more minutes, so you add a tablespoon of butter and keep stirring, so much that the oats are losing their bite. You want to let it go: Noah. The oatmeal. Whatever remains of your and his life. You want, more than anything, to get dressed and leave the house and let him pick up the rest of his belongings without you there—any self-respecting woman would. But you can't stop stirring and tasting and hoping he'll show up hungry or, at the very least, feel enticed by the scent of spices inundating the kitchen.

When he shows up, he stretches out his left arm and offers a side hug. But you wrap your arms around his body, lingering long enough to feel his warmth. A loop plays in your head: He is here. He is real. He is here. He is real.

He says, "I'm all sweaty."

You don't care, is what you'd like to say. You want nothing more than to slide your hand inside his shirt and touch his back.

He approaches the stove, grabs the saucepan lid, and stops short of opening it. He looks at you like he knows he shouldn't. He no longer lives here.

There goes your life. There goes your world. If only you could keep it a little while longer. It's precisely these little moments you miss most. Moments so small and unquantifiable they appear insignificant. Moments like pulling up a chair for the man you love, handing him a spoon, and watching him eat something you cooked.

You point to the pot. "Please, help yourself."

You grab a bowl from the cupboard. Chipped at the top, it's the only one left from a set of four you two bought when you first moved in together. You ladle in some oatmeal and top it off with more sliced bananas and set it down on the kitchen table.

One second, you're watching him eat the oatmeal. The next, you're kneeling on all fours on the couch. Noah is thrusting into you from behind. It is not your imagination. You want to look at his face but lose yourself in the moment. He grips your hips tightly and slows down, then pulls out to touch you. He takes deep breaths and paces himself, and you appreciate him for it. He finishes with a loud and angry grunt, and you remain awkwardly pushed up against a pillow, your neck crooked. From the corner of your eye, you see him pull up his shorts and wash his hands in the kitchen sink. His phone goes off, a noise that sounds like an alarm. He mutters something under his breath, then leaves.

The door closes behind him.

You inventory the things he's left behind: magazines and books about veganism, shirts, ties, pants, and miscellaneous shaving products. Noah doesn't need these items. You must be the reason he comes back time and time again. It can't be for the boxes he continues to forget.

THE NEXT DAY Noah calls to apologize. "Are you sorry for leaving without saying a word?" you ask. "Are you sorry for leaving me?"

The sound of his breath is soft. Calm, even. "Please don't do this," he says.

"What is it that I'm doing to you? What is—"

The phone pings as if the call has gotten disconnected. It's hard for you to believe he would hang up.

IT TAKES NOAH a week to call again. He asks if you can stay at work a little longer while he picks up his things. In an effort to preserve some dignity, you don't tell him you've been fired for missing work or that you've been ill and unable to eat for days. Or that your hair falls out in fistfuls, the strands swirling and gathering in the shower drain. Instead you ask, with your splintering voice, when he's coming back. But he doesn't respond. "Noah? If this is your last trip," you say, "leave your keys in the mailbox when you're done."

WHEN NOAH RETURNS, he finds you sitting on the bed. He sits next to you and rubs your back in gentle circles. You cup his face with your palms. The prickly feeling of his beard soothes you. He kisses your hands, and you drop to your knees and shove his penis inside your mouth. He doesn't stop you. Not even as that alarm of his goes off again. He ignores it and pulls your hair into a pony-tail. And you're crying, but you keep going. Slobbering and gagging and nearly choking on your tears. You finish him off and get up to rinse your mouth. You take a swig of the mouthwash you shared and remember how he hates when you put your mouth directly on the bottle.

When you go back to the bedroom, he is no longer there.

"Noah?"

"Noah?"

"Please. Please. Please. Please, please, please, please. Please!"

The boxes he comes for every week are still here, resting against the wall, stacked one on top of the other.

Worry Bees

NEWS OF THE LOCKDOWN ARRIVED QUIETLY IN AN ALL-
staff email. The school where I worked was too broke to
install a PA system, so the dreaded all-staff email is how
word got around that there was a gun in the school. "**NOT
AN ACTIVE SHOOTER,**" the email said, bolded and capital-
ized. "Just a gun," the principal added casually, as if those
words could assuage anyone's anxiety and fear. Jackie,
Christina, and I were in room 222, Jackie's classroom,
where we spent our off period. Her room was a sanctuary. Some Teach for America donors had given her money
to spruce up the space. Jackie spent it on a mini fridge, a
microwave, and a couch we all took turns napping on. On
the windowsill she kept an array of plants that thrived
despite the oppressive heat released from the decades-
old clanking radiators.

I turned to Jackie and Christina. "You guys read this?"

Jackie lay flat on her purple yoga mat, her eyes
closed and brown hair fanned out like a halo. Sometimes she meditated during this hour, or closed her eyes
long enough to recharge before fourth period, when a
meanspirited trio of sophomore girls would call her

"bitch" under their breaths, then pretend they hadn't said anything. For Jackie, new to Newark and new to teaching, it was the cruelest form of gaslighting she had ever experienced. And sure, Christina and I agreed it was definitely bad, but it wasn't anywhere near what Jackie made it out to be. Still, we understood her frustration. I'd suggested she just confront the girls and tell them flat-out to stop calling her a bitch. But Jackie pointed out I looked like the girls: tough and gritty with gelled hair, big hoops, and bright-red lipstick no matter the time of day. I could get away with a clapback or two. Except I knew I wasn't so tough, wasn't so gritty.

"Guess we're in an active shooter drill?" Christina said. "It's a gun but not a shooter? How would they know the difference?" She typed furiously and the angry clickety-clack of her keyboard made it sound like she was composing an eviscerating email to someone, probably our principal if I had to guess. "Don't worry! It's just a gun! Settle your little worry bees because everything is A-okay," she added, mocking our principal's nauseatingly enthusiastic tone.

"Worry bees," I repeated, laughing.

"You know," said Christina, "that little pesky feeling buzzing in the pit of your stomach, telling you to fight or flight."

"Or hide under a desk and hope you don't get shot," said Jackie.

This was how we coped: with irreverent humor, exchanging self-deprecating jokes as if they were gifts. We could have used this free period for something productive, but each day it was harder for us to be productive. It was easier to talk about the latest gossip instead. Like how Ashley (married) and John (presumably engaged) had gotten so plastered they were seen kissing in the middle of a bar last Friday night. Or how Justin, on a dare, at the shindig following the bar, had tea-bagged Pete by holding out his dick and placing his balls—fully extended and not all shriveled, as some of us had bet—right on Pete's forehead.

We didn't talk about anything serious. Not about Jackie popping pills like Tic Tacs, without so much as a wince while she crushed them between her teeth. Or how Christina seemed to have given up on food altogether and was withering to bones right before our eyes. Or how I had gone AWOL, missing half a week of work, only to emerge from a seventy-two-hour hold as if nothing had happened.

I was nearing my late twenties, burning out from long days of teaching and prepping and feeling like nothing I ever did was good enough. Days went on and on. I'd come in to work before seven in the morning and sometimes wouldn't leave until seven at night. I was overworked and exhausted, and any reprieve usually came in the form of indulgence. It was as if nothing else was left in the world but work, peppered with fleeting moments of happiness. Jackie and Christina were not from the Ironbound, so once their Teach for America commitment was over they could move on, spend their lives doing bigger and better things, as they often fantasized out loud. They had no ties to the city. But I was from here. And I wasn't taking the LSATs or MCATs. This job, in this city, was not a pit stop for me. It was all I had.

The day I'd checked myself into the hospital had been as ordinary as any other. I had been to Brooklyn to get drinks with friends, trying to dispel the aimless *want*, the *ideation*. On my way back to Newark, while waiting for the train, I spotted a dead rat, its carcass flattened against the tracks. Its torso had lost its shape. Not much left of it but the semblance of a head and a tail. I moved closer to the yellow painted line at the edge of the plat-form, envying the creature's rest. It didn't have to fend for itself anymore. It didn't have to fight to exist.

Standing there looking at the rat, I'd wanted to jump. I thought I would do it this time, but I managed to resist the desire. Instead I went home and soaked cherries in rum for an upside-down pineapple cake, drank the resid-ual juice straight from the can, tipped the bottle of rum into my mouth, drank some of that, too, and baked a cake as "a gesture of love for myself" as my therapist had once suggested. I waited, staring at the oven for twenty-eight minutes till the timer buzzed. Taking the cake from the oven, I flipped it over, then dug into it with my hands, bringing warm chunks to my mouth like a desperate animal. A trickle of sugar and butter ran past my wrist, into my sleeve, and down to my elbow. I ate and cried, but the *want* didn't go away, so as a bigger gesture of love for myself, I called for help.

There was no good way to explain the malaise. There was no good way to explain that my life felt like an endless performance, always a few degrees shy of truthful. I was trying my best to be happy. It's what I had told my mother when she asked me what I had to feel sad for. What was there to be so miserable about? As if I needed to be given a reason. I was trying my best, that was the truth. I didn't need a reminder to count my blessings. And I didn't need to feel guilty about my stable job, my health insurance, and my decent salary. I didn't need a reason to be sad.

I LOOKED AT the old clock hanging in the back of Jackie's classroom. It had been at least fifteen minutes since we had read the email. A thought began to buzz inside me: What if there was a real shooter? What if I died in here?

Her classroom was so quiet that I could hear the clock ticking—a rare occurrence. This wasn't our first lockdown or our school's first foray into dysfunction. There had been lockdowns, bomb threats, and even break-ins. Once during winter break someone was found squatting inside the school. But in all those scenarios there had been so much noise. This time the school was silent. We couldn't hear a peep from the classroom next door, no footsteps echoed down the hallway, and no one's phone notifications echoed through the walls. Nothing.

"Remember when I confiscated Brianna Johnson's phone last year, and she threw her binder across the room and said, 'Catch a bullet, hoe'?" I paused, then continued, "Well, here we are. Maybe I can stop paying my student loans once and for all."

Jackie laughed nervously. Christina simply stared at me. The silence that followed felt even more harrowing than the silence I'd been trying to break. I offered a half apology and reminded them that this probably wasn't a real active shooter situation. Jackie sat up, dug her hand inside her pocket, and pulled out a pill that she swallowed without any lubrication. She handed one to Christina, who swallowed hers as well. I watched and understood. We all had our ways of dressing our wounds, of pacifying what ate away at our souls every single day.

Jackie stood up, rolled up her yoga mat, walked to her closet, and placed it inside. "Well, this closet is full of textbooks from before we were born, so we can't even fucking hide."

The thought buzzed again. Where would I hide if I needed to? What if I did catch a bullet? What if it pierced the glass window and shattered my collarbone? The school had yet to make any statements on social media, which only meant the situation had not been resolved, which meant the police had not been called, which meant the administrators most likely thought they could handle it themselves, which meant it was probably serious enough, which meant they were strategizing, which meant they didn't want to cause a panic. I refreshed my email: no updates. Whatever was happening was still happening. For a brief moment I considered whether I needed to text my mother.

Jackie turned to face me. "Should we make parting videos of ourselves?"

Christina shook her head in disapproval. "Jackie," she muttered. "What if it's a serious lockdown?"

"I don't think so," said Jackie. "They would have let us know it's a real emergency."

"Would they?" Christina rubbed her temples with her index and middle finger. "Michelle?"

I didn't know what to tell them.

"I think I need to leave," Christina said. But before she could stand up, Jackie said no.

"Hush," I said. It was becoming increasingly clear that we'd been reckless about this whole thing. "Maybe we should move toward the far corner of the room."

Jackie and Christina agreed and began to tiptoe their way across the room. We all sat in a circle and instinctually muted our phones.

"Should we be quiet?" Christina asked. "Should we text instead?"

Jackie was growing impatient. She placed her phone inside the front pocket of her denim jacket. "Fuck. Can we just whisper? I can't even look at my phone anymore. Imagine having to sit with your students during something like this."

"I couldn't do it," Christina said. "I would leave. I'm having a hard time keeping my own emotions in check. I don't know how you're so calm, Michelle."

"She's dead inside," said Jackie.

I couldn't hold it against her. Most days I did feel dead inside. "I'm sure it's not serious," I lied.

The day of my release from the hospital, when it had been obvious to the clinicians that I wouldn't hurt myself, I'd prayed all the way to the exit. I so desperately wanted it to be the last time. At the bus stop right across from the hospital, a woman in a puffer coat locked eyes with me and told me it was the end of the world, that the rapture was coming. She went on about her vision while I searched for the bus schedule and considered calling an Uber instead. In her vision she had seen it clear as day: We would be gassed to death. A glass dome would descend upon the city, encasing us like a snow globe. And we would choke on our own pollution, coughing our lungs out, spitting blood on the ground, and soiling each other's shoes. It was coming. And we need not repent for it. It was too late for that. "What will you do when the end of the world comes?" she'd asked. The question seemed more rhetorical than real. She was going to smoke cigarettes, she told me—one after the other, from the tip to the filter. She'd eat cookies—raspberry Linzers dusted with powdered sugar—even if their little seeds got stuck in the cavities of her worn-out teeth.

I hadn't engaged, but I'd thought about her question. I would call my mother, I thought. I would call her and tell her this was the last time I would plan it. I would say to her I would wait for my day. And I would not entertain the fantasies no matter how intrusive the thoughts; I would work harder to not think about it again.

"What if this is a wake-up call?" Christina asked.

"What the fuck was that?" Jackie said.

A *pop pop pop* traveled through the hallway, followed by a ruckus of laughter that echoed. There were screams coming from the classroom next door, but they quickly subsided, as if whoever had screamed realized they needed to shut up.

Footsteps sounded in our direction and someone pulled at the door handle, rattling the door with force and laughing maniacally. Jackie screeched, and Christina reached over and covered her mouth. I covered my own mouth, then stared at Jackie. Tears rolled down her face. She kept hyperventilating and reaching for Christina's hand. But Christina pressed on, holding her even tighter, so tight that for a moment I feared she would suffocate Jackie to death.

I sat still, stunned by the beating of my own heart. A pounding that made my chest hurt. I uncovered my mouth, and briefly my hand brushed against the floor, registering the warmth of something liquid pooling near me and spreading toward my leg. I felt a shrill forming in my throat and covered my mouth again with my now wet hand. Trying not to heave, I turned to Christina and Jackie. It wasn't clear which of them had peed on the floor. We remained still, huddled in a puddle of urine.

"Do that shit again," a disembodied voice yelled.

The *pop pop pop* returned just as loud as it was before, followed again by laughter.

"We gotta go," another disembodied voice said, this time distinctively feminine. "Fuck this school!"

A foul, sulfuric smell seeped into the room. The voice faded into the distance, and after a moment of calm, I crawled to the door and slowly lifted myself up to the glass window. There was no one. The hallway was clear except for a discarded box of firework poppers left a few feet from the classroom door.

It was a prank.

I inhaled and exhaled, then crawled to Jackie's closet, where she kept her yoga blanket. I took the blanket, then crawled back to them. I unfolded the blanket and draped it on top of us, building a fort to shield us from absolutely nothing. The bell rang, signaling the beginning of the next class period, but everything around us remained silent and still, so I didn't say a word. Instead I basked in the relief that I made it through the hour. That I was still alive.

A Grieving Woman

THE METAL STOOL IS COLD, SO ALANA SWINGS HER LEGS
to the rhythm of a rock song playing from a digital juke-
box. She wants a third drink, but the bar is crowded.
Bartenders move left and right, swiping credit cards and
counting dollar bills. Her eyes shift between the woman
sitting next to her and the wall behind the bar. She likes
the woman's plum lipstick and dark eyeshadow. She
likes her distressed denim jacket and the wide silver ring
around her thumb. An older woman. Alana likes that too.

The wall behind the bar is a blackboard, the menu
written in chalk, listing snacks and desserts. The rest of
the space is taken up by a selection of beers from small
breweries in the Tri-State area.

Alana shifts her body so that she's facing the woman.
"What are you drinking?"

"I'm not sure yet," the woman says. "What do you
recommend?"

"Well, that depends on what you're in the mood for."

Alana scans the features of the woman's face. She's
attractive, not that it matters. Tonight any warm body
will do.

"I'll have whatever you have," the woman says.

She smiles, gazing briefly at Alana's cleavage. Alana pulls her stool closer and orders two whiskeys on the rocks, though she knows she shouldn't drink any more. On the walk over from the train station, she'd smoked a joint. And before that she'd taken one of the sedatives prescribed to her after the procedure. But she is grieving.

Alana doesn't hear the woman's name. She barely registers that the woman is a bank teller who experiments with various forms of art, including painting and sculpting. The woman tells her she's learning how to weld. She can make beautiful pieces with scrap metal: wind chimes, bookends, picture frames. Alana nods and puts on her customer-service face. Practiced and fool-proof, it can deceive anyone. Her disinterest will never be obvious to the woman, whose enthusiasm intensifies each time Alana smiles. The more the woman speaks, the more Alana feels the passing of time and the way small talk drags and seems to last forever. Alana just wants to fast-forward to the part when she feels better.

What brings Alana back to the present is the woman's hand on her lower back, tentative at first and then asser-tive, applying just the right pressure. When the woman leans in, Alana kisses her, pushing the weight of her face onto her. The woman kisses her back, and Alana slides her tongue inside her mouth. For those few seconds she forgets about the stabbing pain in her lower back, the droning noise in her head like the hum of an engine.

It's a desperate kiss, more intense than it needed to be. The woman abruptly backs away, excusing herself, and Alana hurts all over again. She would have taken the woman home, or anyone willing to follow her back to Newark, across a river and two trains away.

She pretends not to be embarrassed. It's obvious the woman isn't coming back, so she walks to the bathroom and splashes cold water on her face. There are trails of toilet paper on the floor and drops of urine on the toilet. She squats, making sure she's not touching the seat. She gets lost staring at the stain on her panties; it's like an inkblot that resembles a human face. A grieving woman will sometimes see things that aren't there.

ON THE TRAIN platform, Alana's eyes trace each letter in "DOWNTOWN." The weed makes her notice how the droplets of water trickling from the ceiling echo when they hit the floor; how the rats scurrying on the tracks move erratically in zigzaggy lines as they nibble a variety of crumbs and filth; how the man on the platform is thin but has broad, slumped shoulders, as if he's spent a lifetime doing physical labor.

The man's right foot is propped on a bench as his long fingers awkwardly loop his shoelaces into bunny ears. He seems as drunk as she is. She moves closer, past the column blocking her view of the man, and inadvertently steps on the yellow line. A draft of cold wind hits her in the face. The man glances up and waves at her, his hand swaying side to side almost mechanically. She waves back.

Three weeks ago she'd been sitting in her living room unsure about the baby. Even though she had always felt the parenting urge, that bellyache instinct that made some women coo, the man she'd been sleeping with wasn't her boyfriend, or someone she'd ever imagined as the future father of her children. So she'd scheduled the appointment.

The drive to the clinic was filled with moments she could only describe as fortuitous. Every light green, every neighboring driver polite. Getting there could not have been easier or more convenient.

She'd arrived an hour before her appointment and parked toward the back of the lot. Removing the keys from the ignition, she'd placed them in her coat pocket.

First came the sedative, then the stainless-steel speculum, followed by the suction. She'd squinted. The light from above had spread like a sunburst. Before she knew it, the procedure was over. She was given some prescriptions to fill, which she did at the Walgreens on Ferry. But as soon as she'd arrived home, she'd begun to panic. What if that had been her only chance? She thought she'd feel relieved, but instead she'd felt a gnawing. Acid bubbling and burning her throat. That all-too-familiar fear of having to spend the rest of her life alone.

On the platform she can't quite make out the man's face. When their eyes meet, a black marker falls from his hands. It is one in the morning and they are the only ones waiting for a train. She looks at the wall behind her and sees a fresh graffito of a stick figure holding a briefcase.

"You did that?" she asks.

He takes a step back and reaches for a backpack on the ground. Something's off about his face, she realizes.

Something akin to ignorance, or innocence, or confusion, or inebriation, plays across it. But there's also this
sense of familiarity, like she's seen his hooded eyes and
his dark brown skin many times before. She notices he
is beautiful.

"Did you draw that?" she asks again.

His clothes are filthy, patches of crusted dirt coat-
ing his kneecaps. There is a dark stain on the collar of
his crew neck T-shirt.

"I'm sorry," he slurs in an accent that sounds faintly
Dominican. She wonders if the man is even fluent in
English. She could try speaking to him in Spanish, but
that would require effort. And whether he speaks or not
is beyond the scope of her concerns.

She stares at the man and thinks that he's not like
any man she's touched. She wonders if he's noticed her
the way she's noticed him. Does he think she's beautiful? Does he notice her full breasts peeking out from her
tight button-down blouse?

When she asks what his name is, he takes another
step back. She extends her hand and says, "My name
is Alana." He takes her hand and shakes it firmly, then
aggressively. He's swinging her whole arm before she
realizes this is a game that amuses him. She notices
the man's backpack on the floor, then the tattered yoga
mat and cardboard box underneath it. "Are you taking
the train? Do you need to go somewhere?" she asks,
though she's already figured out he has nowhere to go.
Then the idea flashes in her head like the shadow of a
cloud passing through. Before she weighs it, or gives it

any consideration, she's already invited the man to come home with her.

He shrugs.

She thinks about it: this man, this stranger, possibly unwell, possibly lost, possibly not in control of himself, coming with her to her place. A stupid idea. But she is so sad it doesn't even matter. "Just for the night," she says.

The train stops and they walk to an empty car. She leads and he follows. They sit side by side, the ride eerily quiet. They watch the doors open and close. 110th, 92nd, 86th, 79th, 56th, 42nd, 34th. Neither says a word.

The man dozes off and rests his head on her shoulder. His warm breath smells like alcohol. She takes his hand onto her lap and examines his fingers, the rings of dirt that surround the nail beds. She leans closer and sniffs his hairline. He smells faintly of fresh-cut grass and sweat.

AT HOME HE sits on the edge of her forest-green couch and clutches his backpack on his lap. This isn't some shelter where he has to guard his belongings, Alana thinks. She wishes he would loosen up. Here he's surrounded by soothing neutral colors. The decorative pillows are simple and plush. The throw blanket is soft. The pothos and the spider plants and the peace lilies are not only lush but also purifying.

She sits next to him and stares at the gray hair at his temples and the black hairs folding smoothly over his forearm. She wonders if the man is hungry. Her hands are steady enough to make him a meal.

When she touches the stubble of his chin, he smiles. This is weird, she thinks. This doesn't make any sense. She wants to care for the man, use him to fill the hollow spaces of time, to shorten the distance between sunrise and sundown, to carve a wider gap between control and insanity.

She walks to the kitchen and pours herself a glass of wine. She hands the man a glass of wine too. From her bedroom she brings him a fresh towel. Tells him he can shower, leave his clothes in the washer until morning. He nods and accepts the offer.

She's content watching him slide each leg out of his dirty jeans. She's content admiring the contours of his body and how his penis is long and slightly curved. She wants him on top of her. She wants him to insert himself like a hook and pull something from the walls inside her on his way out—something bulbous and painful like a tumor, something that doesn't belong. But it doesn't take long for her to remember that there is nothing there.

So I Let Her Be

THE DAY MY MOTHER RAN AWAY FROM HAPPINESS, I STOOD with her in the bedroom-turned-studio that had become her everything. She ripped off a piece of packing tape, her sharp nails puncturing adhesive and plastic. Crouching, she placed the tape over the flaps of a cardboard box, then smoothed it out. "This one's ready to go," she said, pushing the box with her bare foot. I watched the box glide across the polished floor. When it arrived at my feet, I picked it up, balancing it on my right knee for just a second. The box was heavy.

My mother, too, was heavy, only with sorrow. Her studio had unearthed a better side of her, a happier woman. I wanted to keep that version. But ever since the incident, she'd made up her mind that it all had to go: the canvases, the tripods, the resin molds, the full-body mirrors, the vanity, the negligees, the makeup.

I tried to stop her. I tried to tell her I didn't care that my classmates had seen pictures of her naked body, that I, in fact, loved her nude photos. I was neither embarrassed nor humiliated. I didn't care what anyone said. I admired her art. The way it changed us, how it brought our lives from a blur into sharper focus. But my mother put my needs above her own, and my classmates' taunting at school, like the constant prick of a needle, wasn't something she could ignore.

She reached for another box and folded it, then secured the bottom with packing tape. "Hand me the bubble wrap," she said, and I grabbed it, absentmindedly popping a few of the bubbles before she shot me a look.

"Let's get this over with," she said.

"Here," I said, handing it to her.

My mother and I were living off a settlement she had received from a malpractice lawsuit. It was enough money. It allowed her to work odd jobs and do some freelance work. She'd been a dog walker, a babysitter, a server for a catering company, a Zumba instructor, a valet, a tutor. But none of these jobs made her happy. She'd spend her free time looking for love and companionship. It was as if she was perpetually homesick for something.

As if they were made from a mold on some assembly line, each new boyfriend was a replica of the last. Fast-talkers, Don Juans and Casanovas from every corner of the Caribbean. My mother loved those men: muscular and dark with well-kept beards and blue-collar jobs. Men who'd break her heart.

Before the nude photographs, before she found something she loved other than me and the men who cycled in and out of her life, my mother had struggled to get out of bed. She'd argued she was fine, but her body kept a tally of the losses. Each relationship subtracted something from her, leaving less and less behind. I surveyed the damage: the bloody cuticles, the clumps of hair in the drain, the pervasive smell of sweat that clung to her.

She had begun by photographing herself. Awkward shots in front of a mirror before upgrading to more serious poses, better cameras, and a tripod that allowed her to set her arms free and in motion. She'd once said the glossy sepia prints of her naked body made her feel wanted in ways she had never known.

Sometimes all she'd wear was a crown of flowers. She'd pose in front of her camera with her curls draped over her breasts, her hands folded, covering a patch of pubic hair. In that room full of light, against a backdrop of pothos ivy and string-of-pearls, she looked ethereal. A modern-day Eve in a Garden of Eden. She'd print these images and then collage them onto stretched canvases.

She sat on the windowsill and shook her head. The studio was now in disarray. Even her stool and dressmaker mannequin were on the floor, as if she had thrown them in a fit of anger.

"What about all the money you spent on all these things?" I asked.

"What about it? It's my money. I can spend it how I choose."

"That's not what I meant." I said, gesturing with my hands. "I mean, is this really necessary?"

"I know what you meant." She walked over and kissed my forehead. "I'm too old to be doing this anyway."

The morning of the incident had been like any other.

My mother and I walked toward the train station. We stopped for pastries. I had a small coffee while she ordered an espresso. I turned on Van Buren, and she continued a few more blocks south.

But then I made it to school, and the moment I set foot in homeroom, I heard the whispers, murmurs crawling on my skin like a trail of ants. There were glances, too, defiant and transgressive in their persistence. A boy whose name I never cared to know was the first to say the words out loud, delivered with a deadened expression: "I saw your mom's website."

Taking down the website did nothing to dissipate the lingering fallout. The pictures had multiplied like a virus and taken over my life. For weeks it was all I heard about. I'd become the girl whose mother was rumored to be a porn star. Random classmates would ask me if I sold photographs, too, if I photographed my mother, if she photographed me. I ignored the comments. I was a senior planning to attend art school. My mother and her projects were living testament that art healed. I had no choice but to let it go. For the first time in a long time, my mother was happy.

I grabbed a piece of tulle from the floor. "Can I please keep this?"

My mother had glued crystals and pearls to it. The day of that shoot, she'd draped yards of the fabric over the floor. She'd lain naked on top of it with her legs closed and her arms folded against her chest. She'd guided me as I wrapped her body. A mummy shrouded in a bride's veil, she looked beautiful.

She looked at me. "Fine," she said. She understood how much the fabric meant to me.

I ran to my bedroom with the tulle under my arm. Folding it neatly, I placed it inside a drawer, then took a deep breath and returned to the studio.

"What is the point in keeping all of this?" she asked. She grabbed a silk kimono hanging from a hook near the window. Balling it up, she tossed it on the ground.

"You don't have to stop. It's over," I said. "Nobody cares. No one is talking about it." I wasn't lying. There were other scandals. Other things people worried about. My mother didn't respond. She reached for another box, then put it back down on the floor.

"What I need is the trash can. Please get it for me," she said with finality. I knew better than to keep pushing.

As I walked to the kitchen, I thought about how sometimes she'd smile in her photographs. Wide smiles that rang true, like she was reliving moments of pleasure. Those pictures she liked to preserve in prisms made of resin. Happy versions of herself fossilized in plastic. Years later she would say that she was never a real artist, that the photographs, the resin arts, and the collages were just silly crafts that got her through a difficult time.

I brought back the trash can and set it in front of her. She reached for an array of knickknacks behind her, figurines she'd kept on the mantel. A ceramic cat, a wooden box where she stored incense, a deck of tarot cards, a collection of alabaster angels, a Magic 8 Ball. She held each item, then one by one placed them gingerly at the bottom of the trash can.

This is what she wanted, so I let her be. I stepped out of her way and leaned against the doorframe. The light filtering through the window illuminated her face. In spite of everything, right before the gloaming hour, in the coral and lavender of the Newark skyline, she was my perfect mother. Perfect, even if once again awash in grief.

This Wasn't Supposed to Happen

IN THE BIBLE, HELL IS A FIREPIT. BUT HERE, HELL IS THE sound of my voice, pleading with Lucía over and over to stop the car and consider that this is a stupid idea. That nothing good will come from this. She makes a sharp left and parks across from the basilica. It is nine o'clock on a Thursday night. There is no one here but us and the gargoyles perched on the towers of Sacred Heart—and God, if you believe in him and his omnipresence.

I haven't asked Lucía if she has a plan. Judging from the rise and fall of her chest, the high pitch of her voice, I don't expect her to string together a coherent sentence. She reclines the seat and covers her face with her palms.

"Andrea," she begins, "I'm so sorry I dragged you into this."

It's a little too late to be sorry. At some point tonight there'll likely be an Amber Alert buzzing every phone within a hundred-mile radius: brown-skinned, curly-haired girl in a 2014 black Toyota Prius. Lucía doesn't have custody of Melissa. Not since the separation and the hearings and the battles after her husband found out about our affair. The kid is strapped into the back seat, wearing the ape pajamas I bought her a couple weeks ago. Apes on skates, apes wearing helmets and knee and elbow pads. I turn the radio to the smooth-jazz station in hopes that the music will drown out the desperation in Lucía's voice. I don't want Melissa to wake up disoriented, asking why her mommy is crying or why she is not yet home with her daddy.

Lucía looks at me. "You hate me now," she says, wiping her nose with the back of her hand. She's a sloppy crier. The wet-shirt, snotty kind.

I tell her I don't hate her. But it is crazy that she picked me up and didn't tell me Melissa would be in the car, and she has no intention of dropping her off at her father's.

For months now she's been struggling with this new normal, with the idea that Joseph is the one who snuggles Melissa at bedtime on most nights. The one whom Melissa cries for when her stomach is upset, when she's dropped a toy, when she wants yogurt or applesauce.

I turn around to look at Melissa. Her lips are parted, and her breathing is a little labored. For a few days she's had a rattling cough that morphs into a wheeze. Had the cough started a year ago, before me, before the affair, Lucía would have taken her to the doctor. I look at Lucía but don't say what I think. I don't tell her she's not a good mother, or even a decent one anymore.

"Can we at least call Joseph?" I ask.

She shakes her head. "It's too late for that. He'll call his lawyer and then I'll never see Melissa. We can't do that."

The "we" goes off in my head like a gong. There is no "we." There was never supposed to be a collective unit sharing common goals. There was me, bored of squinting at a screen and punching keys, of recoiling from every happy-hour invitation, every office-bonding retreat. And then there was sweet Lucía, the office's mom, a woman devoted to her family but touch-starved under the surface.

I sit up to get my phone out of my pocket.

"Where are you going?" she says, her hand on my forearm as if to stop me.

"Nowhere, babe." My phone is wet from the sweat soaking the fabric of my leggings. I wipe the screen with the back of my sleeve.

"Are you calling someone? Who are you going to call?" She swallows and grips the steering wheel a little tighter. I can hear the panic in her voice. "I'm not calling anyone." I put the phone back in my pocket. I take a deep breath and smile. The basilica looms over us. I stare at it and remember a time when I'd dare go inside, and the rays of sun filtering through the stained glass felt like God was shining a spotlight on me. Lucía doesn't like the word "affair." Even though that's how it started before spooling out and tangling into a mess I can't get out of. Before it all began I was bedridden with loneliness, with the realization that my world was an endless loop, moving between work and home and nowhere else. And then the affair came. We started small. Furtive glances across the office's open floor before I kissed her one day in her Prius in a dim parking garage. It was obvious from the start that she was as sad as I was. That she, too, wanted to feel some type of love.

On one of those nights, when we'd kissed ourselves into exhaustion, I asked Lucía if she thought we would go to hell. She was still on top of me, her thighs wrapped around one of mine, when she laughed in my face. "You seriously believe in hell?" She lay down, rubbing the dampness of her body onto mine and kissed a trail from my neck to my navel. I couldn't tell her that hell *had* to be real. That you couldn't hurt people and walk away unscathed.

Lucía turns off the heat and cracks open the window. It is cold outside, but she is also sweating. I turn the heat back on and look her in the eye. "Melissa is in the car," I remind her. She scratches her forehead and exhales.

"Lucía," I add, "Joseph doesn't deserve this."

"He's not a good man," she says. "You don't know what he deserves." Her words, flat and unemotive, ring untrue. We both know she's lying. Joseph was neglectful, sure. He didn't kiss her how she wanted to be kissed. He never made her orgasm. But he isn't a bad man.

"Lucía—"

"I want to start over," she says. "We can start over and be a family. You and me. Melissa loves you, and I love you. I love you so much. And I know you love me, otherwise you wouldn't be here. And we deserve better. Don't you think we deserve better? Don't you want a family?" She rips a hangnail from her thumb but doesn't seem to notice the blood gathering at her cuticle.

If she's come up with a plan, I don't even want to know. I take her hand and place it on my leg. "We will have the family you want," I lie, "but it can't be like this. Please. Let me call Joseph."

Just once, I entertained the fantasy that we could be a family. It came to me like an illustration in one of Melissa's picture books: The Newark sky was a brushstroke of pastels. Lucía and I pushed Melissa on a swing; she flew high, and when she returned to us, we embraced her.

My brief fantasy receded like a wave at the shoreline. After, I never again imagined us together. Truth is, I couldn't be near her or the kid without feeling pangs of guilt. I had played a role in wrecking their lives, and now everything was collapsing on me. For months I've looked, quietly, for an exit sign in the dark. But the more I look to escape, the more Lucía builds whatever is left of her life around me. The glow of that exit sign grows fainter and further out of reach.

The night Joseph found out, he stood below the overpass across from my apartment yelling, right before the PATH train whooshed past. Somehow he had figured out where I live and had seen Lucía and me kissing on my balcony.

Most of what he said was lost to the screeching grind of metal on metal and the conductor announcing the train's arrival to Newark Penn Station. The one thing I heard clearly was that I was going to rot in hell. His words boomed with conviction. There had to be a hell, and it was for homewreckers like me.

Lucía touches the side of my neck with the back of her hand. It doesn't soothe me. It reminds me that we're still here, in this car, deciding, deliberating, waiting for something. This wasn't supposed to happen.

"Talk to me," she says.

"About what?"

"About anything. I just can't stand that you're quiet. You're just sitting there."

"We need to bring Melissa back before Joseph calls you."

"It's not so fucking simple," she argues. She hits the steering wheel with her left hand and accidentally honks the horn. A man stops and stares at us from the distance.

Lucía puts the keys back in the ignition and starts the car. She pulls onto Clifton, heading toward the highway. Through the window I notice the cranes and mounds of sand on the side of the highway. Construction tools illuminated by strobe lights. Once, right at the start, when everything was new and exciting, Lucía and I met at the construction site of the new park across from the Prudential arena. I watched Lucía climb a tractor, her short dress billowing with the wind. Underneath she wore nothing. Her brown skin glowed. She stretched out her hand and pulled me up, then asked me to trace my lips over her C-section scar. I lifted her dress and did as she asked. She wrapped her hand around my ponytail and pulled me away and told me she loved me. More than anything. More than anyone.

It is ten o'clock. We have been gone for one hour and neither my phone nor hers has gone off. The highway is clear, so Lucía steps on the gas as if we've decided on a destination. Her right hand shifts from the steering wheel to her silver necklace, which she tugs lightly. I want to think that we won't be moving much longer. That she is ready to drive back to Joseph's. I don't dare ask.

"Are you okay?" she asks.

"No. I have a headache."

She looks at me, frowning. "I have some water back there." She lets go of the wheel to reach behind her. The car veers a couple of degrees to the right, and my heart jumps. It's obvious Lucía shouldn't drive. But if I take over the wheel, then it looks like I'm in charge. Like I kidnapped her kid.

"Just drive, please."

"Okay, I'm sorry," she says. "Can you just reach and grab it?"

As I fumble for the bottle, I look at Melissa. With her head resting on a travel pillow, she looks just like her mother. I try to imagine what she will look like ten years from now. I don't see it. When I shift my gaze to Lucía and try to imagine her in the future, I can't picture her either. I want to memorialize her in my mind's eye, but I can't see her past this very moment. I grab the water as I struggle to conjure a different, newer version that isn't the frazzled, broken woman sitting next to me.

I take a sip. "Do you have Advil?" I ask.

"Maybe in my bag?"

I reach for her purse and swivel my hand inside it. I feel the travel-size bottle of Advil, the ridges on the lid.

"I can't find it," I lie. "Can you pull over at Wawa so I can buy some?"

"Can you just wait a little?" She shifts her gaze to me and merges into the middle lane. The car behind us passes, honking his horn as he drives away.

"Okay, okay, I'll pull over," she says.

Her face creases as she pulls into the right lane. I feel pain shooting up my chest and sweat pooling at my neck. I want out more than ever.

Except for a couple of truckers, the lot is empty. I pull my phone from my pocket and place it on the dashboard. I don't want her to think I'm going to call Joseph the moment I get a chance. She looks at the phone and doesn't say a word. She doesn't need to. I can sense her relief from the way she caresses my thigh.

"Do you want anything?" I ask.

She thinks about it. "I don't know. Get some snacks, I guess." She grabs my phone off the dashboard and tries to hand it to me.

"I don't need it. I'll be right back."

I get out of the car and walk across the lot. I don't look back at Lucía. I don't look back at Melissa.

Inside, the lady at the register gives me a nod and I wave hello before counting to ten and opening the door on the opposite side of the store. There's a Walmart straight ahead, the parking lot packed as always, with a line of shipping containers along one edge. The lights are dimmer over there. Just behind them are the marshes. Tall grass, seemingly sprouting out of nowhere.

I begin to run, my feet stomping against the pavement, until the ground beneath me is no longer concrete. Until my feet sink into the earth and the water reaches my knees.

The Fake Wife

I MET THE FAKE WIFE AT AN ALL-INCLUSIVE RESORT IN Boca Chica. Back then she wasn't the fake wife. She was Marisa, a bartender—curvy and wide-eyed, with a heavy pour on the rum and the smiles.

I had agreed to come to the bachelor's party with my boys only because my best friend Marcos was getting married and I couldn't say no. We joined the Marines a couple years after high school, served six years, and lived through the deaths of our mothers and a few of our closest friends. In the Marines we had bounced from station to station, so in the two years since my service ended, I'd lost interest in going places and being around people. I traded that life for the solitude and predictability of a job at the auto shop, where every day was more or less the same. Yet there I was, on the first day of a weeklong vacation, inconspicuously—or at least I thought so—staring at this woman, her long curly hair tangled inside big gold hoops.

She worked in one of the resort's onsite bars, the one closest to the beach, a palapa with a wraparound deck and TVs broadcasting boxing and other sports most hours of the day. Out of all the bars inside the resort, this one attracted the most men: single men looking to talk to the bartenders, married men seeking refuge from their children and wives. I, too, was looking for refuge from my crew, so I'd find myself at the bar, watching the waves crash and recede over and over.

She was beautiful and spoke English with ease and comfort, entertaining every conversation, whether it was about sports, games, gambling, food, politics, or even history. It was no surprise when men dropped twenty-dollar bills into her tip jar, which she pocketed swiftly, a smile on her face.

That evening, while I waited at the bar for the other guys to come down for dinner, an inebriated older man a few stools away reached across the bar and touched a strand of her curls. She frowned and backed away without saying anything. Her obvious discomfort was unsettling, and it bothered me more than it probably should have. Before I knew it, I had gotten up from my seat and walked over to the man. "You gotta go," I said, with a firm hand on his shoulder. I stood next to him and stared until he knew I meant it. Tall, burly, and intimidating wasn't my favorite version of myself, but the occasion called for it. He got up and pushed his stool in, mumbling as he walked away. I returned to my seat, a burst of adrenaline radiating through my chest. Marisa walked over and asked what my name was. "Chris," I said. She looked around as if to check who else had noticed the situation. She thanked me, and I nodded, redirecting my gaze to the TV behind her.

I kept coming back to the bar and finding her there,

sometimes in the mornings and afternoons, sometimes at night. It seemed she worked every shift, changing her pastel uniform to match the time of day. It didn't take long for us to greet each other with a sense of familiarity. I wasn't frequenting the bar looking for her, though that's what Marcos and the rest of the boys assumed. I didn't correct them. With the pretense of wanting to sleep with her, I didn't have to join them in their itineraries. I had become a regular, sitting in the same spot, ordering the same drink. We talked about the local baseball leagues and the weather. When the crew would return to the bar for shots and it was evident to her that I didn't want to keep drinking, she made me mocktails and poured water in my shot glass. When it was too busy or when men were too insistent, she looked at me and sighed, as if I were a safe place to unload some of her frustration.

"I can take you to go get real Dominican food," she said the morning of our third day at the resort. "It's not inside of a resort, you know? If you want." I nodded and took a sip of my passionfruit juice. It wasn't my first time in Boca Chica, so I knew where to find real Dominican food. We had been to the island before. For one, it was affordable. And as my boys liked to put it, you could pay to play. I didn't know if Marisa was that kind of working girl, so I hesitated before saying yes. I wasn't looking for a sex worker.

She asked me to meet her outside the resort on the busy main strip after her shift ended. She didn't want her coworkers to see her leave the property with a guest.

We decided to get some fried fish on the other side of the beach where the locals went. She said she would have taken me somewhere else further into town had she left work earlier, but someone had called out and she had accepted a shift. She really needed the money. She was saving everything she earned to move to the US.

She walked alongside me, pointing to a few works of art outside a souvenir shop. "You see that doll without a face? That's a Dominican artisanal craft," she said so proudly. I couldn't help but find her irresistibly cute. She explained the faceless dolls were built that way to represent the multiethnicity of the country.

Vendors and passersby waved at her. It seemed everyone on the strip knew her, and those who didn't turned their heads in her direction anyway. Men stared at her shamelessly, not even pretending to be looking elsewhere. Marisa kept pulling her shirt down and rearranging her purse as if trying to cover more of her body.

We sat on some plastic chairs near the fried-fish vendor. She ordered for us, then insisted she'd pay. I declined again and again, but she explained that she wanted to thank me for my gesture a couple days ago. So I let her.

Dominican music blared from a nearby speaker. People flocked to the strip. Women dressed in short, tight dresses, accompanied by distinctively foreign older men, cradled bottles of beer in the crooks of their elbows. They laughed, drank, and entertained these men. Palm trees swayed with the wind, and I began to get lost in Marisa's world. She talked about the hotel and the nonstop grind of her job. She asked me about my life in the United States and if I had lived anywhere else, and how those places compared to America. She spoke as if we had known each other for a long time.

"Newark can be very congested and polluted," I said. "Sometimes at dawn, a stench rises into the air. Toxic fumes, I guess. Parking is a nightmare too."

She laughed. "Sounds horrible."

"It is sometimes."

She nodded sympathetically. "Are people poor?"

The question gave me pause. "Some people are. But most people are okay."

"Sometimes I'm not okay here. Sometimes it's very hard for me."

I didn't press on because I knew what she meant. The expectations that tourists placed upon women like her. She told me how, growing up, school hadn't really been an option, though it was all she'd wanted. It reminded me of my mother, who had given birth to me when she was seventeen, who regretted having dropped out of school all her life. She wanted me to go to college, if only so she could live vicariously through me.

Marisa spoke with such longing, the fried fish on her plate growing cold, the plantains becoming hard and nearly inedible. She apologized for oversharing. "You have that face," she said, "the kind of face that makes people want to tell you about their problems."

On my walk back to the hotel, I thought about the intimacy that we had shared, and I cherished that moment of tenderness. I couldn't imagine what it was like to be her, but I knew what it felt like to be in a place you did not want to be. My time in the military had felt that way. I hadn't wanted to be there, but I didn't feel I had much choice. Sometimes working at the car repair shop felt much the same way. For years I had been saving money, waiting for the opportunity to branch out on my own. But I knew we were in no way the same. I was not a woman slinging drinks across from hungry dogs who salivated at my every turn.

ON OUR FOURTH night, my buddies continued to party as if they hadn't partied at all, and I joined them, even though I didn't feel particularly festive. I owed them that much. They boasted about the women they'd met the past few days we'd been in Boca Chica. Women who'd slip naked into the jacuzzi. Women who'd come upstairs to keep them company through the night. They ragged on me and asked me if I'd been keeping busy too.

After rounds of shots and beers, once night fell, we walked over to a bonfire at the beach. I saw Marisa among a group of women standing near the fire. She wore a short green floral dress and looked more relaxed than she did at the bar. More beautiful than ever.

I kept sipping my rum and Coke, watching her from a distance, but at some point I lost sight of her. I was disappointed that she had left before I could offer to buy her a drink.

I walked away from the bonfire, kicking sand with every step. I passed palm trees and hammocks, and other parties where men and women danced to the rhythm of dembow. And suddenly, right as I was giving in to disappointment, there she was inside the gazebo, leaning on a wooden beam, hiding away from the crowd like a wounded bird.

"Everything okay?" she asked me, as if she were still serving drinks behind the bar. She smiled a tired, forced smile like she was running out of gas. Perhaps this, too, was work. I didn't know how to respond, so I smiled back and pointed up at the sky, as if I had something insightful to say. Something impressive. I kept my eyes on the sky, then pointed at a cluster of stars I couldn't even name. *Corny ass*, I thought.

I knew about cars. I knew about sports. I knew about history. I knew about the service, and beer, and architecture. Women sort of escaped me. I hadn't dated since I'd divorced my then wife shortly after the end of my service. Marisa made it easier for me by pointing up to the sky and naming the stars herself. Not their actual names, but the names of her dead. A laundry list of women who'd been looking out for her.

"What are you looking for?" she asked.

"What am I looking for?"

"Yes. What are you looking for in life?"

The question loomed over me for a moment, and I wondered if she had meant it rhetorically or something.

"You want a wife?" she continued, and I guffawed, slapping my knees and all.

But she was serious. "I'm looking for a husband. A business friend."

"A business partner?"

"Yes, a business partner."

She told me she would pay me ten thousand dollars if I married her and helped her get a green card. There was a kind of hunger I recognized on her face. Something painful and sincere, like she'd been treading water, swimming against the current for far too long. It made me feel like a life raft. A way out.

AFTER THE END of my service, I decided not to reenlist, mostly because my mother was dying and I wanted to spend some time with her. But shortly after I came home, she passed, leaving me grief-stricken and confused. In all those years of service, I had forgotten that death was mundane and ordinary. That it happened to people in their sleep, on their beds, while they sat watching TV on their recliners.

Without my mother, I was alone. What made her loss more bearable were her rent-controlled apartment and a few thousand dollars she had left in the bank—money I hadn't even known she had; money saved for me.

I began to spend more time at the auto shop, taking things apart and reassembling them, rote movements that kept me from drifting. Being underneath a truck, or tucked inside the hood of a car, was soothing; it's you and you alone, left to assemble the puzzle of machinery, to repair parts without feelings or expectations.

Years had gone like that. And I just wished I had enough money to have my own shop, to do things my way. Something small, just enough work for me to live comfortably.

IN BED THAT night, I kept thinking about Marisa's crazy proposal. It was the sort of thing that only happened to *others*. But there I was, stretching with my feet up against the wall, considering it in earnest, thinking through the details and logistics.

I knew a few people who'd done it successfully. This and other forms of fraud. Couples whose circumstances were suspicious right off the bat: gaps in age and attractiveness that were sure to have raised red flags. The more I considered it, the more I thought we could get away with it. She was younger than me, but not significantly so. And I was a former military man who had been married once. We were both attractive and would look like a typical couple. We could even look real. As far as sham marriages went, the odds were in our favor.

Except, I didn't know her enough to trust her. But then again, she could have said the same about me. She, born outside the US and paying thousands of dollars, was the one for whom everything was at stake.

WE HAD AGREED to meet under the same gazebo early the next morning. Resort staff, dressed in sky blue, walked around the beach picking up loose cigarette butts and other garbage. Marisa wore tight jeans and a white T-shirt that clung to her body, and I wondered what time her shift began.

She retrieved a small notebook, barely bigger than her cell phone, and wrote the date on one of the pages. She took a deep breath, then explained this would be a long-term investment.

"We have to be careful because they catch us," she added.

"Yes, we could get caught," I said, sort of trying to correct her. "Where did you learn English?"

She rolled her eyes, as if the question hit a sore spot. "Does not matter."

"But it does. I'll have to know every little thing about you." I knew that much about the process.

She was measured with her words, careful even. It inspired confidence but also made my heart rush with trepidation. The same feeling I'd had after enlisting with the Marines and realizing I had made a commitment I couldn't just back away from.

"Listen," I said, "I'm still thinking about it."

I didn't ask her what a girl like her must have done to save ten thousand dollars, or how many years it had taken her. I didn't know enough about the country or about the town to understand why emigrating to the US was the right investment. But if millions of people risked their lives to do it, who was I to question her choice? She was smart. She was clever. She had obviously thought this through.

I thought about the money she was offering. The money my mother had left me wasn't enough to buy my own shop. As hard as I worked, it was difficult to save ten thousand dollars. The arrangement was risky, but it would help me too. And the burden of risk was on her. Not me. I would take my American citizenship to the grave with whatever privileges it afforded me.

WHEN I TOLD her I'd do it, she said she wanted to do as much work as we could before the end of my stay at the resort, so we met again the following day. She had a list of questions written neatly on flash cards. She wanted to know everything about me: my medical history, how many women I'd slept with, the brand of my toothpaste, the frequency of my haircuts, the food I ate, the porn I watched, my spending habits, my bowel movements, how many cigarettes I smoked.

She wanted a crash course, a master class on what it was like to be me. And I answered all her questions, because in my thirty years of life, no one had ever shown that much interest.

She wrote down my answers in Spanish, in shorthand. At first the exchange was methodical. I was strictly answering what she asked. But later in the morning we began to walk toward the main strip, where she bought me coffee. Her hair swayed with the morning breeze, revealing the sharpness of her jaw and her glistening skin. She nodded as I talked, looking me in the eyes. For a moment I forgot this was work. Feeling as if I'd been floating on a lazy river, I kept talking, letting the gentle current push me along its winding shape. I told her about my first heartbreak, the girl I'd married straight out of high school and predictably divorced, the time I got so angry I punched a hole through the drywall, my mother's death, the father I barely knew, the siblings I rarely saw, the loneliness that had crept up, filling up the crevices of my mother's absence.

I MADE IT back to Newark and waited a few weeks before sending off any applications. Though I had agreed, I wanted to see how the arrangement would play out. As I expected, she was consistent, texting frequently and intimately, playing the roles of friend and lover.

She'd grown up near a river, where she learned to fish using cast nets. She'd never owned a pet—not because she didn't want one but because she had never spent time around an animal she didn't have to eat. She'd attended public school, but the busy tourist strips were her best education. She learned English from tourists. All her life she had been preparing for when she would leave the island.

She had thought of everything. She would get a job at a salon in the Heights, close enough that she could split her time between her cousin's place and my house in case we ever needed to prove that we were still living together.

Every night on the phone we exchanged personal details: a childhood anecdote, a joke, a secret. Once when she was twelve, her mother, who'd struggled with addiction, took her to a stranger's hotel room and left her there with no explanation. The man hadn't expected Marisa to be so young and, upon learning that she was twelve, stormed out of his own room in outrage. Marisa had sat on the edge of the man's bed, frightened but resolute to never return home. She'd bounced from one church to the next, spending time with Jehovah's Witnesses, Seventh-day Adventists, and Pentecostals, anyone who was gracious enough to open their doors.

I shared secrets of my own. How I'd shoplifted and exchanged food stamps for money. How I'd hustled anything I could get my hands on, how my mother had survived a heart attack and made me promise I'd find some direction.

It didn't take long before I wanted to hold the sound of Marisa's voice. Once during our routine conversations, I asked her if she'd be afraid to leave it all behind.

"I have family in New York, remember? I'm not alone." Her voice cracked. She paused, then continued, "My cousin, she is waiting for me there. She just graduated, and she's going to help me get my university diploma in a few years."

She yawned into the phone. "We should stay on the phone for a few more minutes," she added.

"Take me to bed," I said.

"You are. On the pillow next to my face."

"What does your pillow smell like?"

"Shampoo. Suave Coconut. Write that down."

I laughed. On the phone her slow breathing evolved into gentle snores. I didn't want to, but I pictured my chin resting in the crook of her neck. The scent of coconut lulling me to sleep. It felt so real I could smell it.

I FELT LIKE I was on a bicycle riding down a steep hill, gathering speed, panicking, flailing my feet, seeking some friction, the hot pavement chafing the soles of my shoes. I needed to slow down. But even though I knew this, standing in the self-checkout lane at ShopRite, I couldn't help but scan the coconut Suave.

At home I washed my hands with the shampoo, bringing my palms to my face. I inhaled the artificial scent and felt myself spiraling for a moment. It was as close as I could get to her for the time being and that was okay. People settled for the next-to-best thing all the time. I texted my dude Marcos and asked him if he wanted to get a few drinks at the bar. His brother Bernardo had done something like what Marisa and I had planned. Except it had happened long ago, before the Twin Towers collapsed, when immigration laws were a little more lenient. *Bring Bernardo. I got some questions*, I texted.

As I got ready, I caught myself looking at my watch and calculating the time difference, picturing where Marisa was and what she might be doing. For a moment I considered texting her to let her know I would be out with my boys and not to expect a good-night phone call from me. But again, I was being fucking ridiculous. We weren't dating and I had zero obligation to let her know my whereabouts, or to expect her to let me know if she had made it home safely.

At the bar, after a beer and a shot, Marcos and Bernardo told me that I needed to calm down.

"Did you even tap that?" Bernardo asked.

I shook my head. "No. I thought that was the thing you weren't supposed to do."

"I mean, why not?" asked Marcos. "As long as you wrap it up. Just don't hit it raw, you know? You're not trying to father somebody. I mean, unless you are.

Bernardo here can tell you." He put his arms around Bernardo, who laughed as he shook his head.

"You got your wife pregnant?" I asked.

Bernardo looked at me. "You mean the fake one?"

I nodded.

"Yeah. But it's all good. Not a big deal."

"Not a big deal?" said Marcos. He motioned to the bartender and pointed to our empty bucket. She nodded, opened the fridge behind her, then walked over to us, three beers in each hand.

"That's just a bad investment, my guy," Marcos continued. "She paid *you* for papers and now you're paying *her* for child support. Bad business. But let me shut up, though. I love my nephew."

Maybe it was the Coronas talking, or maybe neither Marcos nor Bernardo felt any significant way about the whole thing. Bernardo had divorced his fake wife but they remained on amicable terms. After all, they had a child. And she had gone on to marry an old boyfriend she hadn't seen in years. The love of her life, as Bernardo put it. Supposedly he had been waiting for her all along. For a moment I wondered who might be waiting for Marisa. Who was this cousin, anyway? Marisa never said much about her. She hadn't shared whether they'd grown up together or how often they saw each other, or anything, really.

We kept drinking. Bernardo said immigration wouldn't come knocking unless we were stupid and something about us was glaringly questionable. I feel reassured in our plans, though still slightly uneasy at the realization that life was complicated and plans could change.

I felt the need to pull away, to gain some sort of control over my life. As I left the bar, I thought of reopening the dating apps. Maybe what I needed was to hook up with someone, to remind myself that I was not in a committed relationship but rather a business transaction. Who was to say Marisa wasn't doing the same? But right as I turned the corner to my street, my phone pinged.

It was Marisa. She had just sent me a nude.

Real talk, I ran home. I sprinted down the block and up the steps to my apartment and sat on the edge of my bed. I opened the picture, wishing I were sober, wondering if in my drunkenness, somehow, I had conjured her naked body out of thin air. But it wasn't my imagination. She had indeed sent me a photo of herself in front of a full-length mirror, her cell phone in front of her face, concealing what I could only hope was a smile. Black panties with lace detail. And her full breasts, exposed.

I shook my head in confusion, but only for a moment. The picture had me thinking about sex with Marisa in a way I hadn't quite thought of it before. What I felt wasn't just arousal; it was a familiar surge of anticipation. When I closed my eyes, I didn't just picture her breasts. I pictured my hands cupping them. I pictured myself kissing them. The thoughts and feelings were too concrete for my liking. I wasn't entertaining a fantasy, which could have been easy to dismiss. I was entertaining a possibility, which implied a certain type of hope.

The naked picture made me think about the reality that she would really be coming. She was coming home to me, to my city, to my house, in her regular clothes, outside of the fantasy of a beachside resort, into my world.

The picture fucked me up.

I held the phone in my hand and replied with the fire emoji. Like a fucking idiot. Soft-ass, corny-ass mother-fucker. But then again, what was I supposed to do? Reply with a dick pic she definitely had not asked for? I knew better than that.

The seconds that followed felt like an eternity. I wanted to know what it meant. What did she want me to do with this? How did she want me to proceed? Was I not supposed to jack off to it later?

The next day we texted each other the usual hello. Nothing more. All day I was shaking off intrusive thoughts of her naked body. During my lunch break I submitted the rest of the paperwork for the marriage and her arrival. I ordered some new shirts. A pair of cream pants. A white guayabera. An outfit that would look appropriate for a tropical wedding and showed that I cared. I booked my flight to Boca Chica for my beachside wedding with my fake bride. My heart fluttered and fluttered and fluttered. And there was nothing I could do to stop it.

THE PROCESS INVOLVED unreasonable amounts of paper-work. A logistical nightmare that made the ten thousand dollars Marisa had offered feel like a skimpy amount in comparison to the level of effort it took to sort out all the details. Still, I navigated through the applications. If anything, they served to tame some of my excitement. I was a helium balloon, buoyant with happiness. The logistics were the hand holding on to a string, yanking me back to reality.

She had a plan for how I was supposed to collect the money. As convoluted as everything else, it involved my going to some dude's place. A friend of a friend of a friend would hand me the money. All I had to do was tell him Marisa had sent me.

I didn't ask Marisa how she had made all these connections. We all knew shady people. In fact, some of us were shady people ourselves. When I did ask her why she was giving me all the money upfront, she insisted I needed to get paid so I wouldn't get confused about the arrangement. This was purely transactional.

Outside the building where I was supposed to pick up the money, a group of older gentlemen were gathered on the sidewalk playing dominos and drinking from Styrofoam cups. A man in a blue polo shirt greeted me in Spanish. "¿El esposo de Marisa?" he asked, and I nodded. I would soon be her husband, that was true. He handed me an envelope, then prompted me to count. The money was there. I placed it in my pocket with the intent of depositing it in the bank. But on the way home I stopped at Lowe's and bought a safety lockbox instead. Something about the money didn't sit quite right. As if it wasn't all mine.

At home I stashed it in the safety box and then locked

it. I set the combination to be our future wedding date. I texted her. *Thanks.*

No. Thank YOU, she replied.

According to my boys, Marisa was probably a chapiadora—Dominican slang for gold digger. They had warned me I'd find a lot of those at the beach resort and the areas nearby. Except what I found were people trying to live. Just like the rest of us in the US. Marisa wasn't a gold digger, and the more I thought about it, the more I felt for her. What a risk, to put that much trust in a man. All my life, my mom had done exactly that—trust men who'd disappoint her, men who shoved her and pushed her around, men whose niceness and mellow dispositions had expiration dates. I couldn't imagine traveling thousands of miles to be with, arguably, a stranger.

MARISA AND I got married at the gazebo on the beach. Our gazebo. She suggested the place. Not for sentimental reasons, of course. But because it made sense—a small open space near the beach where we could have an officiant, a couple of witnesses, and a handful of guests.

It was a breezy day: low tide, blue skies, picture-perfect. By the time I arrived, the gazebo had been decorated with flowers and white balloons. A couple bottles of cheap champagne rested at a slant in an ice bucket. A dozen flutes were arranged on a silver tray. And much to my surprise, there was even a cake. It was modest, but pretty enough that it would photograph well.

Marisa arrived holding a small bouquet of roses. She wore a simple white summer dress. A white rose was pinned to the side of her hair. Her long nails were painted a soft pink. The faux diamond on her finger caught a flicker of sunlight and beamed true for a brief moment. She looked beautiful and I told her so, choking on the words. She looked at me and smiled.

We held hands, proclaimed our vows, and kissed for the first time. A short-lived kiss in front of people I did not know. A kiss her friends made sure to capture from several different angles.

If you didn't know what you knew about us, if you just looked at the photos, at the smile stretching my face taut, at the way her head tilted back mid-laugh, you would assume it was real. You would even root for us.

We kicked off our shoes and posed for a few more iPhone photos in front of the beach. Marisa moved my arms and directed me, choreographing every pose. We turned to face away from the sun while her friend took pictures. She showed us her phone: Waves crashed behind us, white, foamy, and effervescent. Framed by a couple of palm trees against the backdrop of the orange setting sun, we looked like we were living the best day of our lives. "Wow," Marisa kept saying, her face gleaming with satisfaction. I wanted to ask the friend to please send them to me. I wanted to keep those photos.

When her friend walked away, Marisa hugged me. "Thank you," she said.

"Do you want to change and go out to dinner?" I asked. We hadn't made any plans for the evening. But it seemed silly and even suspicious to go off on my own the day of our wedding.

"Yes, now we celebrate. But I'm not paying." She laughed, but I knew she was serious. As modest as the whole ceremony had been, she had to spend a few hundred dollars on the officiant, the champagne, the cake, and the dress.

We had dinner at a small restaurant across the Malecón. Afterward we strolled down the busy strip. She pointed at an ice-cream shop, her favorite.

"Are there good ice-cream shops in New York?" she asked. I wanted to correct her. To remind her that I lived in New Jersey. But I then remembered Dominicans used "New York" and "New Jersey" interchangeably. It was silly. But coming from her, it was quite endearing.

"We go all out," I said. "You haven't lived until you've had a sundae. Not like the day of the week. Sundae as in S-U-N-D-A-E."

She stopped in the middle of the sidewalk and smacked my arm. "Now, how do you know I don't know what a sundae is?" She stared up at me, and I couldn't help but take note of just how much shorter she was. How I could scoop her up, sling her over my shoulder, and run with her.

She broke her serious look with a smile. "Just playing," she said. "I didn't really know what you were saying. In my head I said, 'Wait, what? The day of the week is an ice cream flavor?'"

"Still, I probably shouldn't assume."

She hit the side of my arm again. "Why are you so serious? Always 'sorry this, sorry that.' Just be funny. It's okay."

207

I nodded, feeling like I could suddenly drop my shoulders. "I went to the ice-cream shop you like during my last visit. Their only toppings are cherries and chocolate syrup," I added dismissively. "Just wait until you fly home and you try *real* ice cream."

We walked back to my hotel room, stopping to take a few selfies along the way. Upstairs, I offered her the bed. I would be fine with the chair. She said there was no need for that, and I proceeded to overanalyze her words. Did that mean she wanted me next to her? What if we brushed against each other in the middle of the night? What if I held her?

I made her a drink and then another. She talked about her dream of owning a hair salon. I told her there were a lot of Dominican hair salons back home. She had shared this plan before over the phone. But hearing it in person was different. It made her vision all the more real: A franchise specializing in curly hair. A brand she would grow across cities and states. She spoke fast, bouncing from one idea to the next. I couldn't see her face in the dark, but I imagined her eyes were wide, matching the chirpiness of her voice. She was a dreamer and a planner. And as she spoke, I found myself rapt—I could see her dreams and felt an undue sense of pride in her, for all she had done so far to get herself here. And then it hit me that the telltale sign of love is when you want the other person to win. I wanted her to win. I needed her to win because I loved her.

SHORTLY AFTER OUR wedding, I flew back home. Marisa stayed, working overtime to stash away as much money as possible before her travel paperwork came through. The day I called her to tell her it had, she screamed so loud I felt my ear throb. Her breath quickened with excitement. Months of planning—years, even—had led to this moment, and I could feel her anticipation thousands of miles away.

"How cold is it now?" she asked on the phone. I texted her a screenshot of the weather report. It was the middle of November. She would arrive in a couple of weeks to what I considered to be a mild winter. It was thirty-eight degrees Fahrenheit. I googled the Celsius conversion, but she remained silent on the phone.

"I don't understand how cold that is. Hold on," she said. I heard what sounded like flip-flops shuffling against the floor. "I'm walking to the refrigerator." She laughed. "Okay. I'm here. I put my hand inside the freezer. Is that how cold it is?"

I joined her in laughter before the sobering realization that she really couldn't gauge how cold it was. She had never experienced the biting sharpness of winter chill, or numb toes from wearing too-thin socks. She had never slipped on ice and fallen flat on her ass on the edge of the curb, or done the fidgeting-and-jumping dance to stay warm standing on the platform, waiting for a train.

"You'll get used to it," I said, reassuring her that we all hated the cold but had learned to deal with it, as you do with everything else.

The following morning, I spent hours looking for a coat. Something warm and comfortable to wrap her in when I picked her up from the airport. I also chose gloves, a hat, a scarf, and a pair of fleece-lined boots. Good quality stuff I thought would last her a while.

ON HER ARRIVAL day, it snowed—not much, but enough to stick to the ground. I got to the airport early, parked in the lot, and waited by the pickup area. A crowd of travelers exited through a door and rushed past me. I scanned the crowd, swiveling and panicking at the thought that I wouldn't recognize her, or that she might hop in a cab and go elsewhere. It didn't take long before I started to feel dizzy. The wheels of a stranger's suitcase ran over my feet. I watched it happen, unable to move out of the way. I crouched, afraid I would pass out at any minute.

I sat on a bench, taking deep breaths, gripping the coat I had bought for her. What if she hated it? What if she ended up hating me?

I rested my hands on my knees and tried again to slow my breathing. I thought of my mother, how she'd never let me play with anyone else's toys, how she'd never even let me drive her car, how she'd insisted I never get used to enjoying what wasn't mine.

We had planned everything through her arrival, anticipating as much as possible. But we hadn't talked much about what would happen once she had made it to the States. Eight months of my life, that's how long we'd been talking and working toward this. The realization that we were nearing the end of the transaction weighed on me, as if someone had placed a car battery on my chest.

When I looked up, she was there. My fake wife, standing in front of me. Her mouth was open and she was trying to catch snowflakes on her tongue. She looked silly and sweet, bubbling over with cheer.

"I'm here," she kept saying. "I'm here."

I got up and hugged her, lifted her off her feet, and spun her around. I allowed myself a few seconds of unbridled, conscious joy. The kind of joy you admonish yourself for. The kind of joy you *have* to feel before the clock runs out. I draped her coat over her shoulders and watched a smile spread across her face.

On our way to the car, she held on to my arm and took small, unsure steps on the fresh snow.

"I'm not going to let you fall," I told her. Still, she gripped me harder. When we made it to my car, she looked at the clock, dumbfounded, then checked her phone.

"It's so dark," she said. "It's not nighttime. Why is it so dark? Is it always like this?"

"This time of year, yeah." It must have been an alien world to her, marvelous and disorienting.

I imagined she was tired, but I still drove her around the city and turned my head every now and then to see the expression on her face. At times she looked amazed but also sad.

When I opened the door to the apartment, I was overcome with a pang of insecurity. My place didn't exactly look like a home. There was a mason jar full of old cigarette butts on the windowsill, stinking up the living room, and I realized the fridge was completely empty, save for a few cans of High Life.

"Don't worry. I'm going to help you," she said, standing on the tip of her toes to give me a kiss on the cheek. She said her cousin in the Heights would pick her up in a few days. In the meantime we needed to go on a date here and there, add to the portfolio we'd compiled of all these fabricated moments.

"Just in case immigration snoops around," I added.

OVER THE COURSE of several days, I watched her burn her arm on the radiator, set off the smoke detector time and time again, and refuse to drink water from the faucet. She cleaned around the clock, picking things up faster than I could put them down. In my broken Spanish, I would tell her to take it easy.

Days turned into weeks. The house smelled like fresh sazón. She'd blend garlic, peppers, onions, and herbs. The whirring of the blender was a noise I wanted to get used to. We ate plantains a lot. Mashed, twice-fried, stuffed, boiled, baked. She kept finding new ways to cook them.

If the months leading up to her arrival had dragged, the time we spent together zoomed right past us. Our nights were filled with laughter, giddiness, and self-discovery. I'd come home and find her swaying her hips to bachata. She'd extend her hands, and I'd move forward, sometimes stepping on her toes. She'd complain but keep dancing, her hand on my lower back pulling me closer, a big smile stretching across her brown face.

We took trips to Home Depot and Lowe's. We bought plants for the kitchen windowsill. We found a cypress bookshelf at an estate sale and dragged it inside the apartment. She claimed it might be haunted but didn't care anyway. It took us several trips to the bookstore and the Lutheran church's weekend book sale, but we filled it up with titles we wanted to read together.

Two months went by and the cousin in the Heights still wasn't ready to take her in. I felt like I was holding my breath. I thought at any moment I would find her cousin downstairs waiting for her. I told Marisa she could stay for as long as she wanted. After all, we could try to be seen by more people, spend more time building the veracity of our marriage.

She wasn't homesick often, but one day I found her crying on the couch, the evening news playing in the background. I surfed channels until I found a soap opera in Spanish. I draped a blanket over her and made her chocolate-chip pancakes, which she had grown to love. Then she asked me if I wanted a girlfriend. The question took me by surprise. I lowered my gaze. I hadn't thought about anyone else but her.

"It's okay if you do," she said.

"I don't. Why? Do you want a boyfriend?"

She shook her head as if it were an accusation. "No."

"Are you happy here?" I asked. She ran her fingers through my hair, and I wrapped myself around her like a life preserver.

"Yes," she said into my ear.

That night, she began sleeping in my bed, and I

vowed not to initiate anything. We had gotten so close I'd begun to think heartbreak was an imminent threat, and I wanted to avoid it as long as possible.

We didn't really talk about her cousin. Not because I didn't want to. Marisa just seemed to evade my questions about her, offering as little information as possible, giving me generic responses I could do nothing with. When I asked if they had grown up together or how often they saw each other, she didn't answer. Her name was Alejandra. That much I knew. She had gone to college and earned a doctorate degree, a tidbit of information that made Marisa swell with pride.

Whenever Alejandra called, Marisa would run to the bathroom and turn on the faucet, as if trying to muffle the sound of her voice. She spoke to Alejandra in a fast, almost coded Spanish, and I gathered that I needed to give her space, even if I was dying to know what they talked about. Even if, somewhere inside me, their secrecy didn't sit well.

"Invite her over," I said one afternoon. I stood over the sink, rinsing dishes and placing them in the dishwasher. Marisa sat at the table painting her nails a bright shade of red.

"Yeah, one day," she said.

I turned to face her. "Why not this weekend?"

"Well. I think she's very busy."

Every attempt to bring up Alejandra yielded the same result. I let it go, worked hard to rid myself of the discomfort. My curiosity was tinged with jealousy and the suspicion that something was amiss. But I had no right. No right whatsoever to feel any sort of way. Except, even as I would say that to myself, Marisa and I grew closer, blurring the lines of whatever it was we had going on. This platonic romance. This connection disguised as transactional friendship.

OUT OF NOWHERE, Marisa showed up at the body shop. My buddies stared at her as she walked toward me, their heads swiveling in the direction of her ass.

She told me she had walked all the way to the shop, past the Manischewitz factory and the underpass where kids raced at night—the industrial backroads of the neighborhood. She asked about the smell. "It's called Jersey," I joked, but she didn't get it. She said we needed to talk.

We went to a tapas restaurant where we shared small bites and a pitcher of sangria. The whole time I felt my chest rise and fall as if I'd had three espressos.

"What did you want to talk about?" I asked.

"Us." She reached across the table and held my hand. Her eyes lingered on my face, and for a moment I felt warm. She got up and kissed me on the mouth. Our second kiss. Except this time I hadn't expected it, and it wasn't being recorded for posterity.

"You know something? Maybe we should just have fun tonight," she said.

I didn't argue. We kept drinking, and by the time the server brought the check to our table, I was seized with anticipation. Suddenly my apartment, merely a mile away, wasn't close enough.

We didn't even make it out of the garage. In my car she unzipped her pants, grabbed my hand, and placed it in between her legs, guiding my fingers, telling me when to speed up, when to slow down. I touched her, kissing her lips and neck, holding back the urge to tell her I loved her. She climbed on top of me, and I reclined the seat. It started fast and ended even faster, with her slumped over my body, her wet lips pressed against my neck.

HER COUSIN ALEJANDRA began to call more often and at all hours of the day, or sometimes in the middle of the night. Marisa began to ignore her calls, forwarding them to her voicemail. At times she would turn her phone off, cutting herself off from the world.

Then the phone calls became fewer. Alejandra had relented, but only for so long.

One day she showed up at my door unannounced: the mysterious cousin whom I had wanted to meet in person for so long.

I invited her inside. But she stood on the sidewalk, holding on to the rail at the bottom of the stoop. She wore slacks and a blazer, an untucked white blouse, and heels. I didn't know where she worked, but I gathered it was the kind of place with a formal dress code. She looked professional, even if her eyes were red and her hair was slightly disheveled.

She sniffled, then tucked a strand of hair behind her ear. "Can you tell Marisa to come outside, please?" Her voice cracked, and it was evident she had been crying.

"Is everything okay? Why don't you come inside?"

She shook her head. "No. Can you just—"

Marisa ran up behind me. "Alejandra—" she said, before stopping herself short.

I turned around and saw Marisa was covering her mouth, already crying. She was barefoot, wearing shorts and a cropped T-shirt. Not enough clothes to step outside into the frigid cold.

I looked at Alejandra, then looked back at Marisa. It felt as if someone had punched me in the gut, knocking the air out of me.

I walked down the stairs and ignored Marisa calling my name. I speed-walked to the bar down the street, shoving my hands into my pockets. It was cold. So cold I couldn't think about anything but the frigid wind numbing my skin. I didn't have my wallet, keys, or phone. But the folks at the bar knew me well enough.

At the bar I ordered a beer, feeling the chokehold of my stupidity loosen. Alejandra wasn't family. Marisa and her were something else. Where had they met? At the resort? How long had this been going on? It began to make sense: her desperation and desire to leave her town. Her constant remarks about not being able to be herself. But then why did she stay with me for as long as she did?

What we were building had felt real.

Speculating only made it worse, but I couldn't help myself, couldn't stop poring over all the events that had taken place, how close we had become, how everything about our lives resembled love.

I had a beer and then another, enough to ease my frustration. It wasn't my place. Perhaps I'd believed too much in our fake relationship. Who was I to make a judgment about her life or her choices? I was only passing by. I was only playing a role.

I ambled my way back home, wiping my tears with the back of my hand. Before I reached the knob, Marisa let me in. She had been waiting. I imagined her forehead against the door, her eyes fixed on the peephole. I was surprised to find her still there.

Upstairs, everything was left as it had been. Her clothes were still in the closet, her suitcase still stored away. I didn't want to assume. I didn't want to hope. In my haze I took stock of the home we'd made. The decorations, the artwork on the walls, the books we both now read.

We didn't say a word to each other. I went to bed, too tired and too heartbroken to argue, or to even ask questions. The less I knew, the better. I lay there on my bed, planning to call out of work, pack a duffel bag, and disappear for a few days. The thought of having to save face terrorized me. I couldn't fathom another performance. Minutes went by and I began to drift into an uneasy, light sleep.

I tried not to listen for her. I didn't want to hear a noise and suddenly find myself making meaning of it, spinning a narrative to make myself feel better. Perhaps that was what I had been doing all along, spinning a narrative to soften the blow of unrequited love.

But at some point in the middle of the night, I awoke

to the creak of the bedroom door and the slow shuffle of her feet, the unmistakable sound of her slippers against the hardwood floor. Perhaps Alejandra was back, waiting for her downstairs so they could slip away once I was asleep.

I waited for the glow of the light bulb to pry my eyes open. I waited for the stretching, unsettling noise of her suitcase zipper to make my skin crawl. I waited for the click of the front door to break my heart.

Instead I felt her arms around me, spooning me, her breath softly caressing my neck, and her tears trickling down my skin. I didn't speak and neither did she. In some absurd, irrational way, we fit, like the interlocking bones of vertebrae. I cried, too, then turned around, wrapped my arms around her, and stroked her back over and over until she drifted into sleep. There she was, right next to me, and I couldn't help but wonder if we could just be. I kissed her forehead. "I love you," I whispered.

"I love you too," she whispered back. I took a deep breath and felt the violent beat of my heart, angry fists punching me from the inside, slow into a normal rhythm. I closed my eyes and wished for another day.

And another, and another, and another.

Credits

The World as We Know It (p. 55). Originally published as "The End of the World as We Know It" in *Michigan Quarterly Review*, volume 60, issue 2, April 2021.

Bear Hunting Season (p. 73). Originally published as "The Widow" in *The Brooklyn Rail*, October 2022.

What Is Yours (p. 93). Originally published as "That Which Is Yours" in *Cagibi*, issue 9, January 14, 2020.

Jászárokszállás, Hungary, or Newark, New Jersey, or Anywhere, USA (p. 105). Originally published as "Jászárokszállás, Hungary, or Anywhere, USA" in *HAD*, edited by Aaron Burch, January 20, 2020.

Love Language (p. 129). Originally published in *The Pinch*, volume 41, issue 2, October 13, 2021.

I'll Give You a Reason (p. 141). Originally published in *American Short Fiction*, August 3, 2021.

Something Larger, Something Whole (p. 147). Originally published in *Abstract: Contemporary Expressions*, edited by JL Jacobs, September 16, 2019.

A Grieving Woman (p. 165). Originally published in *Tahoma Literary Review*, issue 21, August 9, 2021.

Acknowledgments

To my loving Gregory, who has been my rock and sanctuary—thank you for your patience, understanding, and endless love. You have believed in this dream as if it were your own. You kept me grounded and focused all these years. Your belief in me has been a driving force behind this book.

Estoy profundamente agradecida a mi familia—Mami, Papi, Joel, Carlitos, Tía Dora, Tío Micky, Mami Elena, Pamela y Annalise—por su amor, apoyo, y aliento. Su fe en mí ha sido mi luz y guía. Los quiero mucho.

Michael Lolkus, Bobby Rubin, DeriAnne Honora, Morgan Babst, and Megan Holt—thank you for your encouragement, companionship, and love. Your friendship has been a source of comfort and strength.

To my writing community and friends—Angela Houston, Peyton Burgess, Sydney Rende, Chris Stuck, T Clark, Maurice Carlos Ruffin, Rogan Kelly, Tom Andes, Karisma Price, Kayla Min Andrews, Emilie Staat Strong, Tayari Jones, Deesha Philyaw, Ivelisse Rodriguez, Camille Acker, Amy Dupcak, Henry Goldkamp, Michelle Nicholson, and Lindsay Sproul—thank you. You made this book possible.

I am grateful to my editor, Margot Atwell, for her meticulous attention to detail and commitment to excellence.

I want to thank the Feminist Press team for their commitment to bringing this book to readers.

To the Louise Meriwether First Book Prize judges—Cassandra Lane, Lupita Aquino, Nancy Jooyoun Kim, and Bridgett M. Davis—thank you for championing these stories.

To my Newark writing club and early readers—Vanessa Cruz, Brent Weber, Anthony Francesco, Marta Tchorzewska, Franny Lopez, and Ellen Gagnet—thank you for engaging with my work.

I want to express my sincere appreciation to my UNO classmates and fiction cohort—Marlana Botnick Fireman, Andrew Cominelli, Sophie Nau, Ely Vance, Alex Moersen, Katrina Dahl Vogl, and Natalka Proszak. Thank you for your feedback and support. A heartfelt thanks to my UNO professors—Neal Walsh, Joanna Leake, and Barb Johnson—for their guidance.

This book is a testament to the love, support, and faith of all these wonderful people. I am eternally grateful to each one of them. Thank you from the bottom of my heart.

And to the city of Newark, you welcomed us and gave us a home when we lost everything. My heart will always belong to you.

The Feminist Press publishes books that ignite movements and social transformation. Celebrating our legacy, we lift up insurgent and marginalized voices from around the world to build a more just future.

See our complete list of books at
feministpress.org

Founded in partnership with *TAYO Literary Magazine* in 2016, **The Louise Meriwether First Book Prize** is awarded to a debut work by a woman or nonbinary author of color in celebration of the legacy of Louise Meriwether (1923–2023). Feminist Press is honored to be the publisher of Louise Meriwether's *Daddy Was a Number Runner*, one of the first contemporary American novels featuring a young Black girl as the protagonist. The prize seeks to uplift much-needed stories that shift culture and inspire a new generation of writers.

**The Louise Meriwether
First Book Prize**

THE FEMINIST PRESS
AT THE CITY UNIVERSITY OF NEW YORK
FEMINISTPRESS.ORG